A Horrible Crash of Thunder Split the Sky.

She jumped, and the mug slipped from her fingers and shattered on the hard floor. She looked at it in dismay, then bent to pick up the large, jagged pieces.

Suddenly Grant was across from her, wordlessly helping. They reached for the same piece and their hands touched. Both straightened, the broken mug forgotten. He took her hand in his and looked down at it. Blood came from a small cut on the tip of a finger. His dark eyes held hers as he brought the finger to his mouth and gently sucked it.

Her breathing grew erratic. She wanted to strike him for doing this to her, and yet she didn't move. Abruptly he released her hand, as though he suddenly realized what he was doing, and walked away from her.

Dear Reader:

I'd like to take this opportunity to thank you for all your support and encouragement of Silhouette Romances.

Many of you write in regularly, telling us what you like best about Silhouette, which authors are your favorites. This is a tremendous help to us as we strive to publish the best contemporary romances possible.

All the romances from Silhouette Books are for you, so enjoy this book and the many stories to come.

Karen Solem
Editor-in-Chief
Silhouette Books

BRITTANY YOUNG
No Special Consideration

Silhouette *Romance*

Published by Silhouette Books New York

America's Publisher of Contemporary Romance

Silhouette Books by Brittany Young

Arranged Marriage (ROM #165)
A Separate Happiness (ROM #297)
No Special Consideration (ROM #308)

SILHOUETTE BOOKS, a Division of Simon & Schuster, Inc.
1230 Avenue of the Americas, New York, N.Y. 10020

ISBN: 0-671-57308-X

First Silhouette Books printing July, 1984

10 9 8 7 6 5 4 3 2 1

Map by Ray Lundgren

No Special Consideration

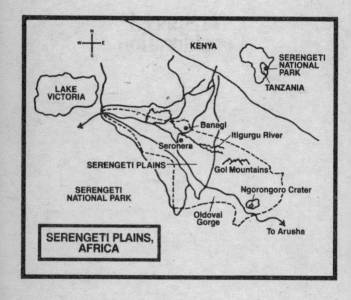

Chapter One

Dr. Grant Adams tiredly pushed the battered bush hat back on his sun-bleached head and surveyed the plain as it stretched before him, his brown eyes narrowed against the harshness of the African sun. It wouldn't be long before the rains came. And with the rains would come the animals, back from their long migration.

This place, so serenely sleeping on the edge of the Serengeti, was intended as a haven for them—a place where they could roam, safe from poachers. A place where he could study them and their habits, treat their illnesses, and learn how to breed them in captivity to rebuild their populations.

But money was tight. He was down to six rangers and one assistant, and it wasn't enough. Not nearly enough to patrol the miles under their protection. The African government gave them all the support it could manage, but money was scarce and needed elsewhere. At this very moment the poachers who took such a horrible toll of the animals every year were rebuilding their hideous death camps as quickly as he could destroy them.

The muscle in his jaw worked angrily. He felt helpless, and it ate at him. He was used to being in control.

With a last look at the vast plain he turned and strode up the hill to his modest stone house. The writer for *Vanishing Nature* was due in a few days. It was his last hope for keeping Banagi going. God only knew what would happen to the wildlife if he had to shut down. If the article was well done, it could mean a tremendous renewal of independent funding. He had already sunk all the money he had into Banagi. . . .

Alexandra Hollister felt a sinking in her stomach as she scanned the dark and sinister place. How had she gotten herself into this mess? And would she ever get out of it?

"Alex? Are you home?" came her mother's friendly voice from the living room.

Alexandra carefully backed out of the oven, distastefully holding a dripping, greasy sponge. "In the kitchen!" she called back, gingerly carrying the sponge to the sink and rinsing it out, her straight nose wrinkling expressively.

Helen Hollister, a petite, elegant woman who looked far younger than her sixty years, glanced from the oven to her daughter in mild surprise. "Cleaning the oven? It must be July." Housekeeping had never been one of Alex's long suits, but at twenty-four she was mistress of her own destiny . . . except for occasional loving jabs from parents and brothers.

She grinned engagingly. "All right, mother. Point to you."

"Where's your housekeeper?"

Alex picked up a towel and dried her hands. "Mrs. Taylor comes only two days a week—and this isn't one of them. Besides, she doesn't do windows or ovens."

Mrs. Hollister perched on a stool and laid her purse on the butcher-block kitchen counter. "I noticed when I pulled into your drive that the mail was here, so I brought it up to the house. It's on the hall table."

"Thanks. Can I get you some coffee?" Alex asked, opening the refrigerator and getting herself a Pepsi.

"No. The last thing I need right now is caffeine."

Alex stopped what she was doing and really looked at her mother for the first time since she'd walked in. Something was definitely bothering Mrs. Hollister. Leaving the Pepsi untouched, Alex raised herself onto the edge of the counter. "Haven't you heard?" she quipped. "Frowning causes wrinkles." Then, more seriously, "What's wrong, Mom?"

Helen Hollister's eyes, as startling in their blueness as her daughter's, were concerned. "I think I've gotten the conservation magazine I volunteer my time to into trouble unless I can come up with a quick solution."

Vanishing Nature was a magazine whose existence was justified by the attention and publicity it gave to endangered plant and animal life around the globe. It survived on donations of money and time. Alex's wealthy parents had always been generous with both.

"You see," her mother continued, "I had what I considered a brilliant idea a few months ago about devoting our entire November issue to the animals of the Serengeti. We found a writer-photographer who could afford to work for peanuts and a wild game preserve that was more than willing to house him and show him around for a few weeks. This particular preserve is run by an Australian veterinarian, and I happen to know he's desperately low on funds. He's hoping the publicity will bring in enough money to keep it going."

"But?" Alex said, proddingly.

"But," her mother said, sighing, "with all the preparations made and his departure scheduled for tomorrow, our man came down with acute appendicitis."

"Ah," Alex nodded knowingly. "And you don't have a replacement."

"We've been on the phone all day, and no one can get away on such short notice." Mrs. Hollister hesitated. "Alex, you're our last hope. You know how I hate to involve you in my projects, but it just can't be helped this time."

Alex had seen the request coming. To be honest, it *was* short notice. She wanted to help, but . . .

"There are problems, Mom," she finally said. "I do political writing and interviews. I've never done a nature piece—and I'm not a professional photographer."

"But you're a wonderful writer," her mother said in an encouraging tone. "You've been published in some of the best magazines in America. And you might not be a professional photographer, but you're a very good one. You have excellent equipment."

Alex slipped off the counter and paced. She *was* a good writer. This would be something different for her to tackle. She sipped the Pepsi. "I guess I could do it. I'm working on a few pieces right now, but the information has already been gathered. I could finish them in my spare time there and"—she lifted an expressive brow at her hopeful mother—"as you know perfectly well, I've always wanted to travel to Africa."

"I should tell you," her mother warned, "that while your travel expenses will be covered by the magazine, very little else will be. We can't pay much."

"Don't try to unsell me," Alex said, chastising her mother affectionately. "I've saved enough to get by for a month or two. Besides, my horizons could stand some broadening. When do I leave?"

Her mother nearly leaped off the stool to hug her. "Thank you, dear. I knew I could count on you." She pulled a manila envelope from her purse and handed it to Alex. "Everything you need to know is in there, but to give you a rundown, your plane leaves Chicago tomorrow afternoon. After various stops and plane changes, you should arrive sometime the next day at a place called Arusha. From the airport there you go to the Victoria Hotel where you'll be met by a guide who will escort you the two hundred or so miles to Banagi. There you'll be met by the Australian, Grant Adams."

Alex pulled the material out of the envelope and spread it on the counter. "Why can't I fly directly to Banagi?"

"You can, of course. But when we made the arrangements, we thought our writer would get a better understanding of the area if he drove through some of the country and spent a night or two in a tent."

The older woman watched the younger. She was so lovely, with that thick, tawny hair and honeyed skin. Alex was an intelligent and resourceful woman, but she was too trusting, her mother thought anxiously. Alex was open and honest with everyone and assumed they were the same with her. It wasn't that she was naive. After covering politicans she couldn't possibly be. But she was too trusting. And one day she was going to misplace that trust and get hurt.

Alex looked up suddenly and caught her mother's worried expression. "Mom?" she asked, interrupting Mrs. Hollister's thoughts. "Is there a problem you haven't told me about?"

Mrs. Hollister started, then smiled. "No. No. Not at all. I was just silently wishing you a safe and uneventful journey."

Alex didn't believe her for a second but let it go. If she was leaving the next afternoon there was a lot of preparation to be done.

Two days later Alexandra's plane landed at Arusha, a small town resting in the shadow of the rough-hewn 15,000-foot peak of Mount Meru. As her flight had progressed, she had become more and more excited at the thought of actually being in Africa, not to mention the challenge of doing an entire issue of a magazine on what she saw.

A taxi delivered her to the anglicized Victoria Hotel, and she had the driver pile her luggage next to the entrance while she strolled to the front desk, where a handsome young African greeted her in impeccable English. She smiled at him. "Hi. I'm supposed to meet a guide by the name of . . ." She checked the slip of paper she carried in her hand. ". . . Kingsley Braeden. Has he been here yet? Actually," she corrected herself, "he would be looking for a man. But I came instead."

He shook his head. "I am sorry, miss, but I have been here all morning and have seen no sign of Mr. Braeden."

Her first disappointment. She wanted to get started as soon as possible. "Perhaps I'm early," she finally suggested. "Do you mind if I wait here?"

"Not at all. And I will be sure to let you know the moment he arrives."

With a sigh, she wandered around the lobby, admiring the old-fashioned Victorian furniture. It was a quaint hotel, rather warm on this hot day. A great wooden fan rotated slowly overhead, silently moving the air around the small room.

She read for a while but couldn't keep her mind on the paperback. Pacing didn't seem to help much either. Three interminable hours dragged by, during which she could feel the effects of jet lag catching up with her.

Her attention was suddenly caught and held by an enormous man, his pale skin flushed from drink, weaving his way into the hotel. A smile curved her mouth when he bumped into a wooden pillar and tipped his safari hat in apology.

But that smile faded abruptly when the desk clerk signaled that *this* was the man she had waited for all those hours. She couldn't believe her rotten luck. An absolutely blotto guide.

After speaking briefly with the man at the front desk, he hulked his way toward her, a perfectly charming smile on his round face. "I hope you haven't been waiting long," he apologized, attempting in a most agonizing fashion to pronounce the words without slurring them. "I had some las'-minute things to do." He weaved, even though he was standing still.

"So I see." Resigned, she helped him to a chair into which he promptly collapsed. She wagged an admonitory finger at him. "Mr. Braeden, you're drunk."

His flushed face filled with indignation. "Tha's not true." Then, relenting a bit, he leaned back in the chair. "Well, maybe just a little."

Alex frowned down at him, wondering what to do now. She could pour coffee down his throat and wait until he sobered up. He was certainly in no condition to do his job at the moment. . . .

But when his loud snoring filled the room, she abandoned all hope of sobering him up any time soon. He was going to be out of it until at least the next morning.

With a sigh that started at her tired toes, she walked to the man behind the front desk again. Wordlessly they both watched the guide's huge belly rise and fall rhythmically. "Any suggestions?" she asked finally.

His smile was sympathetic. "If you don't mind waiting for a day or two, I could attempt to find a substitute guide for you."

"You couldn't find one right now?"

"It is a busy time of year for them," he said

apologetically, though it certainly wasn't his fault.

It was the inaction that bothered her most. She wanted to get on with things.

Then a thought struck her. She knew how to read a map. Surely, if she used comon sense a guide wasn't necessary. She turned back to the man behind the desk. "Instead of finding another guide for me, perhaps you could tell me where I might rent a car."

His eyes widened in dismay. "A car?"

"Or whatever kind of vehicle you think I should rent to get to Banagi."

"Banagi? The preserve?"

"Exactly. How far would you say it is from here?"

He shrugged. "Two hundred and fifty to three hundred kilometers."

"What are the roads like?"

"It depends upon which one you take, of course. There is one much used by tourists. It's condition is . . . passable. Then there is the track. It should be all right now, while it is dry. But it is not very much used. There is little development along it."

She nodded. "I see. And what kinds of things should I buy for the trip?"

"Many things." He ticked them off on his fingers. "A small tent for sleeping. A cot, cooking utensils, food, mosquito netting."

He hesitated as he looked at her standing there, all slender five feet six inches of her, her hair curling softly to her shoulders from a side parting, her dark blue eyes beginning to show a hint of tiredness. She wasn't dressed at all right in her full, gathered summer plaid skirt and white short-sleeved blouse. She looked so . . . feminine. "Miss," he finally said, "my advice is to wait for a guide. Truly, it is the safest way to travel."

A warm smile curved her mouth. He was really a very nice man. "Thank you. But now that I've thought about it, I like the idea of traveling alone. I can't imagine that I'll have any trouble if I'm careful."

He strongly disapproved, but he told her where she could make the necessary purchases and rent a jeep.

A little more than an hour later, map in hand, she was off. She chose the track rather than the paved road because what she was after here was nature, not people. Behind the jeep rose clouds of choking dust, which, before long, was inside the jeep as well. If she kept the windows closed it became suffocatingly hot. If she opened them she drowned in dust. Before long her lightweight cotton blouse was sticking to her back, where beads of perspiration had gathered.

But the discomfort seemed to disappear as the jeep climbed the escarpment of the Great Rift Valley. Time and again she stopped to take pictures that she knew could never do justice to what was there. Below her shimmered Lake Manyara. Mountain slopes thick with forests rolled into the water and stretched so far into the distance they grew hazy.

On she traveled, higher and higher. When she stopped to look behind, she saw the peaks of two mountains in the distance. A quick look at the map told her that one was Meru and the other, the fabled Kilimanjaro.

The higher she drove, the thicker were the forests. The road wound its way through them, and she found it a blessed relief to be driving in the shade for a change. Moss hung from the boughs of the trees like green bridal veils, and shafts of sunlight pierced the open spaces between the leaves and filtered to the ground.

She got a stunning photograph of buffalo grazing in one of the clearings. Calmly they lifted their great heads to watch her pass. It wasn't until much later that she learned the African buffalo was one of the deadliest animals of the Serengeti.

When she finally reached the top, she had traveled nearly eight thousand feet up. It was then that she saw spread out before her, two thousand feet straight down, the Ngorongoro Crater. As she got out of the jeep she couldn't believe her eyes. The Ngorongoro Crater was a huge depression in the earth, at least twelve miles wide, completely walled in and containing hills, forests, and even a lake. Countless animals roamed undisturbed on its floor. This surely should be counted among the wonders of the world.

Reluctantly she got back into her jeep again and bumped along one side of the crater, looking for the first view of the Serengeti Plain. The woman who had rented her the jeep told her to expect it near here.

When she finally saw it she stopped the jeep and sat absolutely still, her lips softly parted in wonder. The plain stretched before her and disappeared into the horizon. There was no focal point, but its very immensity was breathtaking. Heat rose in undulating waves from its surface. To the east, offering one boundary, were the Gol Mountains. For the second time in half an hour, she realized her insignificance.

But time was short. She began the descent to the plains. If anyone had told her that going down would be worse than coming up, she would have laughed.

Well, she wasn't laughing now. The track wound through acacia trees. That was the nice part. Unfortunately, some of the potholes she hit were so large she was amazed the jeep didn't disappear into one of them. The journey seemed impossible, and for the first time she wondered about her wisdom in going it alone on this road rather than following the tourist road. At last she made it to the bottom. She was bruised and a little worse for the wear, but she was there.

She plowed along, seeing surprisingly few animals—certainly nowhere near the thousands she had expected. And then, as it became obvious that the sun was getting ready to set, she pulled over to a friendly looking spot and got to work setting up a camp. Getting the tent up wasn't nearly as easy as the directions said it would be. The cot was worth another ten minutes. By the time she finished, she had just enough time to collect twigs and dried grass to make a small fire and attempt to cook some of the canned food.

At last, able to relax, she sponged herself off with some bottled water while her food cooked, then leaned against the jeep to eat. Alone in the wild for the first time in her life, she was vividly aware of the night noises. They were very loud. And very foreign. Half of her was fascinated, the other half terrified. And she was exhausted. Without bothering to remove her dusty clothes, she climbed onto her cot, draped the mosquito netting around, and fell sound asleep within minutes.

Chapter Two

When she awoke the next morning, she lay quietly on her cot. It was already late. She could tell by the way the tent had warmed up inside. Despite the strange environment, she had slept like a baby and felt wonderfully rested and refreshed. Arms high over her head, she stretched her lithe body before lifting the tent flap and stepping outside. It was another beautiful day. With her hands on her hips, she breathed deeply of the fresh air and watched birds wheeling in the cloudless blue sky.

But there was a major blot on the morning as far as she was concerned. Despite last night's sponge bath, she was still covered in dust. Alex spread the map over the hood of the jeep and studied it. Sure enough, there was a small river near where she was. Quickly she packed up her camp and headed the jeep straight for it. It was larger than it had looked on the map but certainly no less welcoming.

Secure in the knowledge that no other tourists would be anywhere near, she stripped completely, grabbed her soap and shampoo, and gleefully dove into the refreshing water. What a wonderful sense of freedom! Leisurely she washed her hair and soaped her body, then dove repeatedly and paddled around to rinse herself. She loved the feel of the cold water as it glided over her firm body. This was the first time she had ever swum in the nude and she loved it.

In a burst of spray she came up for air, her face pointed toward the sky, her eyes closed.

But her peace and privacy came to an abrupt end. An explosion sounded nearby. Her eyes flew open. Something whizzed past her ear and into the water.

A tall, blond man stood on the embankment with a rifle aimed at her. She froze. She absolutely could not move. He shouted something, but she had water in her ears and couldn't make it out. All she could do was stare at that rifle.

Without warning it exploded again and

something behind her, not twenty feet away, thrashed its huge body in the water. A crocodile! Miraculously her limbs thawed, but even as she struggled to the embankment, panic making her slow and awkward, the man dropped his rifle and hit the water in a racing dive. Within seconds he had hauled her none too gently onto the hard, dry ground.

Glaring down at her with furious brown eyes, he stripped off his wet blue shirt and threw it on top of her. "Put it on," he ordered harshly.

Alex was too shocked to be embarrassed. Silently she rose and slid her arms into the shirt-sleeves. The shirt still carried the heat and scent of his body. "Thank you," she finally managed, though her voice cracked on the words. "You saved my life."

Those eyes of his didn't soften in the least. "And had to kill a croc in the process." He spoke with an accent. Australian, she guessed. "He was where he belonged. What the hell were you doing there?"

She nervously pushed the dripping tawny hair away from her face with one hand and clutched the shirt protectively around her with the other.

"I . . . I was so dusty. I just wanted to take a bath and wash my hair. . . ." Her voice trailed off. It sounded so frivolous now.

"Tourists." He nearly spat in disgust. "I wish I could get every last one of you banned from the African continent."

Alex still felt guilty. Her lovely eyes held a plea for understanding. "Look, I'm really sorry. I didn't realize . . ."

"People like you never do. You come out here for kicks, leaving a trail of destruction in your wake."

"I've said I was sorry," she told him more firmly.

He turned away to lay the rifle on the seat of his Land Rover. He was a tall man, at least six feet three inches. His sun-bleached hair was rather short, with just enough natural curl to hold it in place with a careless attractiveness. His body was lean and sinewy, permanently bronzed from the scorching African sun. He turned back to her with a sigh, running his hand through his thick hair. "I accept your apology," he said after a moment, as though realizing he had been too harsh with her. "But do me a favor and cut over to the main road where you won't get into any more trouble."

"I chose this road intentionally. It goes all the way to Banagi, doesn't it?"

He raised an expressive brow. "Banagi? Why would you be going there?"

She fidgeted nervously, increasingly aware

that all she had on was his shirt. "Van-ishing Nature magazine sent me to do an article on the place." She narrowed her eyes against the glare of the sun as she looked up at him. "You're an Australian. Would you happen to know Dr. Grant Adams?"

His disbelieving eyes slowly traveled up and down her length. She refused to give him the satisfaction of blushing.

"I thought they were sending a man," he said.

"Then you're . . ."

"Grant Adams," he finished for her.

Alex extended her hand. "I'm Alexandra Hollister. And a man *was* supposed to come, but he fell ill at the last minute. I'm his replacement."

The Australian's heart sank. He had read some of the work of the other writer. He was good. With him on the side of Banagi, they had a fighting chance. Instead, when he needed a tank, the magazine sent him a pistol.

Alex, who had always been sensitive to people's feelings, found herself particularly sensitive to his. His disappointment touched her as though he had come right out with it. Automatically her shoulders straightened. "Doctor, I can assure you that I'm a good writer. My mother wouldn't have asked me to take this assignment if she had any doubts about . . ."

In utter resignation, he folded his arms across his bare chest and leaned against the Land Rover. His head moved slowly from side to side. Banagi was lost. "Your mother?" he asked flatly.

Now it was Alex's turn to frown. "My mother works for the magazine as one of their volunteers. . . ."

"So the *real* writer can't make it and some rich lady sends her kid instead. Unbelievable."

"Doctor, I would appreciate it if you would let me finish a sentence without interruption."

He gestured broadly with one hand. "Please, Miss Hollister, by all means."

Narrowed dark blue eyes met and held resigned brown ones. "You don't think I can handle the assignment, do you?" she asked finally.

"That's right," he informed her bluntly. "I don't."

Alex moved to within a foot of the man still relaxing against the Land Rover, her arms akimbo, her gaze clear and steady. "Well you're wrong. And what's more, I'll prove it to you. I'm not some hack chosen on the basis of my mother's social standing or my father's bank balance."

A corner of his handsome mouth lifted, deepening the crease in his cheek. He had to admit she had guts. "Very well, Alexandra Hollister. Let's hope you're right. My life, more than you could ever know, is in your hands." He straightened away from the Land Rover, but his eyes remained on the woman before him. She was one of the loveliest creatures he had ever seen, even with wet hair. Her long, shapely legs seemed to go on forever, and her nipples, hardened from the cold water, pushed tantalizingly against the material of the shirt. His body responded intensely to the sight of her, much to his annoyance. Certainly he wasn't averse to some short-term entertainment, but something told him to go cautiously with this woman. He had a strong feeling that she could turn into one enormous complication. That was something he didn't need. Right now he had two priorities. The first was to get Banagi back on its feet. The second was to repair his broken marriage. He refused to accept the divorce. It didn't matter that Carolyn had given him custody of their five-year-old twin sons. What mattered was the failure. He had come from a bitterly broken home, and he refused to allow that to happen to his sons. They needed both their parents, and he was going to see that they had them.

He came back to the present and the girl standing before him.

"I suggest you dress and give me back my shirt," he said abruptly. "Then you can follow me to Banagi. It's not far."

Feeling dismissed, she walked behind her jeep without another word and changed into a pair of slim-fitting jeans and a fresh, sleeveless pink blouse. This job was going to be more difficult than she had imagined. Not only did she have to overcome the obstacle of writing on a subject foreign to her, she had to prove herself to a very skeptical stranger.

She sat on the open gate of the back of her jeep to put her shoes on. But a strange thing happened when she stood up. Her legs wobbled. She was so unsteady she had to sit down again quickly. Even her hands were shaking uncontrollably.

The Australian came around to see what was taking so long. The minute he saw her condition he strode to his Land Rover and poured something from a flask, then held it to her mouth. "Drink this."

She didn't like the sharp smell. "What is it?"

He cupped the back of her head with one hand, still holding the smooth metal cup to her lips. "Brandy. It'll help."

She wrinkled her nose in distaste but swallowed the whole thing. It burned its way into her stomach and radiated outward. Then the Australian picked her up bodily and put her into the passenger seat of his Land Rover. As she watched, he transferred some of her things into the back of his vehicle. "What are you doing?"

He climbed behind the wheel and started the engine. "Driving you to Banagi. I'll send someone back for your jeep." His brown eyes touched hers as he reached into the back and pulled out a blanket, which he gently wrapped around her. "Your body is having a very natural delayed reaction to almost being a crocodile's breakfast," he told her with surprising kindness. "Try to relax. You'll feel better in a few minutes."

She leaned back in the seat, but relaxing was easier said than done on the bumpy track.

The shivering grew worse, and the more she fought against it, the more her body ached with the effort. But within half an hour it abated. The chill that accompanied the shivering disappeared. She still wasn't feeling one hundred percent, but she certainly felt better. She folded the blanket neatly and laid it in the back.

The Austalian glanced at her. "Better?"

"Much, thank you." She looked around

with renewed interest. "How much longer to Banagi?"

"Half an hour, give or take."

"What exactly do you do there?"

He glanced at her out of the corner of his eye. "Is this an interview?"

Alex smiled, and a dimple played at the corner of her mouth. "Let's just call it an informational conversation."

His eyes returned to the road. "We don't do nearly as much as we'd like to."

"Because of money?"

"That, of course, and manpower. There aren't many people who want to devote themselves to the plain and its animals. They miss the modern conveniences. Mostly," he said as he got back to the question, "we study animals and treat any sick ones we find. We study their breeding practices and pass what we discover along to zoos. But lately most of our efforts have gone toward protecting them. There are so many endangered species out here. The ban on hunting over the last decade means that the price of the hide or tusks or whatever they take from the animals has skyrocketed, creating a booming poaching business."

He glanced at her empty hands. "Do you plan on writing things down as we go along, or do you have an infallible memory in addition to all your other . . . admirable qualities?"

She tilted her head to one side at his sarcasm and studied his clean profile. "I should warn you, Doctor, I bite back."

His smile was lazy and . . . suggestive. "I'll look forward to it, Ms. Hollister."

She shook her head, but her eyes sparkled. "You aren't going to make this easy for me, are you?"

"I can't," he said seriously. "It's not an easy life out here, and you're going to have to take care of yourself exactly the way the rest of us do."

"No special consideration?"

"None. You're on your own. If there are outings you want to get pictures of, you'll have to keep up or be left behind."

"Good." She relaxed comfortably against the seat with a smile of satisfaction. "That's the way I want it."

The Land Rover bumped its way through a quiet, dry Masai village. The tribespeople stopped whatever they were doing to wave. A few miles past the village they crossed a dry riverbed and headed up a slight incline to a stone house. Alex climbed out of the jeep and studied her new home away from home with interested eyes while she brushed down her jeans. It was larger than she'd expected, and more modern. Steps led to a veranda that ran all the way around the house. Comfortable old chairs and a porch swing were strategically placed facing the magnificent view of the plain, interrupted only by an arthritic, thick-trunked tree.

"What's that?" she asked, pointing to a large corrugated-metal tank set some fifty yards from the house and near a compound obviously designed to hold animals.

The Australian followed her line of vision. "A water-holding tank. We collect all the rainwater we can during the wet season and then meter it out to the animals who don't migrate during the dry times."

"I see." She pointed to the dry riverbed. "Does that ever have water in it?"

"In the rainy season."

"How do you get across it?"

"We leave our vehicles on the other side and walk over on a rope ladder that stretches from bank to bank."

Two attractive African rangers approached them, smiling politely at Alex and then talking intently to the Australian in Swahili. She listened in fascination. It was a lovely language, easy on the ear, as were the men's soft, melodic voices.

The Australian responded, then apparently gave them some orders because they climbed into the Land Rover and drove off. He walked quickly toward the house with Alex on his heels.

"What's going on?" she asked.

He stopped and turned around. It was as though he had forgotten she was there. "Oh, Alexandra, I sent the men back for your jeep. It should be here in a couple of hours."

"But what did they say to you?" She wasn't concerned about her things. They'd still be there tomorrow, no doubt.

"One of them thinks he spotted Kabloona's poaching camp thirty miles from here. He can't be sure because he couldn't hack his way into the brush alone. I'm going to find out if he's right."

"How?"

"By flying over it."

"May I come too?"

He looked at her—really looked at her—for the first time since the rangers left. "Haven't you had enough excitement for one day?"

"I told you, I can handle anything you throw at me." She patted the camera case hanging from a strap over her shoulder. "I'm ready whenever you are."

A corner of his mouth lifted sardonically. "All right, lady. You're on."

Instead of going into the house, they walked down the incline and the two hundred or so yards to the flat plain. There, they got into a little dual-engine plane, strapped themselves in, and taxied to a clear area.

The plane bumped over the long, waving brown grass, but the minute it left the ground things smoothed out. Alex had never been a fearless flyer. Something always told her that whatever plane she boarded was the future charred and smoking wreckage that would show up on the six o'clock news. It never was, of course, and once she was actually on a plane she would become fatalistic and relax.

This was different. The plane was small, and she felt as though she had some control over her destiny—which she didn't. But the man next to her handled flying as though born to it. And that in turn relaxed her. She trusted him.

They skirted the edge of the plain, where some of the brush was so thick it shut out the sun. She spotted a lion slumbering in the shade of a flat-topped tree. They were close enough so that she could see its rib cage through the tawny coat.

The Australian followed her worried gaze. "He'll be fine. He's a little hungry now, but as soon as the wildebeest return the king will be king once again."

"I don't know who I feel sorrier for, the lion or the wildebeest."

"Don't feel sorry for either. Nature has a way of balancing the animals' populations. The way things are is the way things have always been and the way they should be. That's something you have to realize if you plan on writing more than an African soap opera."

Alex didn't comment. She was quickly learning that to defend herself against his remarks was a waste of time and energy. The only way to prove herself was to show him what she could do.

Suddenly she spotted some smoke coming from the thick brush. "What's that?" she asked, scooting to the edge of her seat and pointing.

The Australian circled the plane over the area, a frown creasing his forehead. "A poachers' camp," he said finally, straightening the plane and heading back toward Banagi.

Her eyes were still on the puffs of smoke. "How can you tell it's not just a brush fire?"

"If you'd ever seen a real brush fire out here, you'd know the difference. What you see down there now are several controlled small fires."

She leaned back in the seat, her eyes on him. "So what do we do?"

He lifted an expressive brow. "We get in

our Land Rovers tomorrow and chop our way into the camp."

"What time?"

"Dawn."

"I'll be ready." Getting up early was definitely not her favorite thing, but with her reputation on the line she'd manage.

Now it was Grant's turn to refrain from comment. The education of one Alexandra Hollister was about to begin. She was going to discover that the real world was a lot harsher than the one she had been cocooned in for twenty-four years.

When the plane arrived at Banagi, Grant circled low twice to scatter the few herds of gazelle and zebra that had already returned, then set the plane down on a flat stretch where it bumped its way to a full stop.

Grant climbed out and walked around to Alex's side to help her down. With his strong hands at her slender waist, he lifted her to the ground. She looked up at him, her lovely eyes alight with excitement. "Now what?"

A slow smile curved his well-shaped mouth as his eyes rested on her flushed face. Alex's own smile faded at her increasing awareness of his hands touching her. She felt their warmth penetrate the thin material of her blouse, and her heart began a rhythmic pounding beneath her breast. A breeze lifted the perspiration-damp hair from the back of her neck. The light fragrance she had used that morning combined with his clean masculine scent to fill her nostrils. It was a heady combination that intensified her awareness of the man.

Grant's smile faded. He knew what she was feeling because he felt it himself. There was a strong physical attraction between the two of them that he had been aware of from their first meeting. But he could tell from Alexandra's expression that it was only now dawning on her. He moved his hands to her shoulders and with deliberate slowness trailed them down her bare arms, his eyes on her sweetly parted mouth.

Alex's breath caught at the thrilling sensitivity of her skin to his touch. He knew exactly what he was doing to her when his hands made their way back up her arms and slid over her shoulders to her back and down to her waist, then pulled her body tightly against his. The air crackled with the electricity between them.

The roar of a Land Rover approaching at full speed barely pierced their concentration on one another. But the booming African voice did.

A corner of Grant's mouth lifted slightly as the hands that had pulled her so close now reluctantly moved her away. Wordlessly he left her standing there, shaken by the power of her attraction to him, while he walked away to greet the ranger.

Alex took a shaky deep breath and put her hand over her pounding heart. She had a disquieting sense of things left unfinished.

It took a minute, but as soon as she regained her composure, she moved away from the plane to stand next to the Australian. He interrupted his flow of Swahili long enough to introduce her to the ranger. His name was Jundi, and he was obviously a man of some authority. His smile enveloped Alex in its warmth as his meaty hand closed firmly over hers. She sensed his sincerity and liked him instantly. He spoke to her in educated King's English, beautifully and elegantly accented.

Grant's brown eyes touched her. "Jundi and I have some things to discuss that wouldn't interest you. Go on up to the house and unpack. I'm sure your luggage has been carried in by now."

She lowered her eyes, unable to meet his gaze. "I'll do that, thank you." Then she turned to the African. "And I'll look forward to seeing you again and perhaps discussing your work for the magazine."

He inclined his head. Alex started on the walk to the house, her mind in turmoil, unaware of Grant's thoughtful gaze following her graceful movements.

Alex showered and took a short nap, then dressed in a lightweight grape-colored skirt, attractively pleated, and a short-sleeved matching blouse. Evening had arrived and darkness was fast approaching as she walked through the cozy, practically furnished living room and out through the noisy screen door to the veranda.

She leaned on the railing and absorbed the awesome view of the plain as it stretched out infinitely before her, dotted with flat-topped trees and occasional animals grazing on the brown grass. She could easily grow to love this place. It touched a responsive chord in a way no country ever had before—except for her beloved America.

A movement near the animal compound caught her eye. The shirtless Australian, his bronzed torso glistening with sweat, walked toward the house, a shirt carelessly suspended from a finger over his shoulder. He was deep in thought and unaware of Alex as she watched, unwillingly mesmerized by his physical beauty. He had the leanly sculpted body of an athlete. The hair on his chest formed a T, running in a narrow line down his muscled diaphragm and disappearing into his jeans.

She straightened as he approached. He looked right at her, but it was a moment before he really saw her, so far away were his thoughts as he climbed the steps. His brown eyes traveled appreciatively over her freshness. "I'm going to clean up before dinner. You have some time to wander if you want."

"I'll do that, thank you." It took a terrific amount of willpower, but she managed to keep her eyes above his neck.

"But don't wander too far. A lot can happen when you don't know what you're doing."

She nodded her tawny head. Satisfied that she had been warned sufficiently, he went into the house, and Alex relaxed. She tensed so everytime he came near her.

With a shake of her head to clear her thoughts, she put her hands in her skirt pockets and headed down a path she had noticed earlier. It wound its way into some dried-out trees and, without realizing it, she lost sight of the house. There was a round grass hut, unoccupied, just off the path. She had passed it and walked several feet when a hoarse roar sliced the evening air. The lion couldn't have been more than ten feet away. Alex stopped dead in her tracks. Her heart missed a beat, then began pounding again furiously. Operating on instinct more than anything else, her knees trembling, she turned with forced calm and walked to the hut, opened the door, then closed it sharply behind her. Weak with relief that she hadn't been attacked, she pressed her back against it and shut her eyes tightly.

Another roar vibrated the door. She jumped and whimpered softly. "Grant!" she called out. Then louder, "Grant! Help!"

But of course he couldn't hear her. She knew it. The house was too far away. She moved away from the door and paced around the dark hut feeling, ironically, like a caged animal.

She peered through the slits in the walls, but whatever was out there was hidden by darkness. She paced again. "All right, Alexandra Barrett Hollister," she said to herself. "People live peacefully on the Serengeti with those very lions. It's ridiculous to be afraid. Just walk out that door and back to the house."

She lined herself up with the door and took a deep breath, then marched straight up and opened it.

Instantly there was a roar and she slammed the door shut, leaning her forehead on it this time. It was useless. She was stranded for the night.

Forlornly she sat on the dirt floor, her back against the wall, her eyes staring into the darkness. She felt perfectly safe now, but suffocatingly trapped. And hungry. Ravenous.

She forced her thoughts in another direction, to the magazine piece, which was beginning to take on a clear shape. It was going to be a journal of her visit.

In the middle of this, the hut door flew open and a flashlight picked her out of the darkness. If her eyes could have pierced the night, she would have seen the utter relief on the Australian's surprisingly pale face. But none of that was evident in his voice. "Did the thought of eating my cooking drive you in here, or are you just eccentric?"

Stunned by his carelessness, she leaped up and dragged him into the hut, then slammed the door behind him. "What are you doing out there? Didn't you hear the lions? And in answer to your question, I want to *eat* dinner, not *be* dinner."

Grant's strong teeth flashed whitely. "They won't hurt you. And if you're going to be here for any length of time you're going to have to get used to this sort of thing." He switched off the flashlight and walked out the door.

Alex stared after him in disbelief. Surely he wouldn't leave her here unprotected!

Without thinking, she ran after him and walked by his side, stiff with fright. He glanced down at the top of her tawny head, a smile behind his eyes.

"Are they still out there?" she whispered.

"Yes. But as long as we don't bother them or act as though we know they're there, they'll leave us alone."

Alex relaxed. He sounded so sure of himself.

"At least they usually do," he added.

She groaned and unconsciously gripped his arm. "You're a real comfort."

His laugh was deep and soft.

The walk to the house seemed endless. She counted all five of the steps leading to the veranda, relaxing only when the screen door slammed shut behind her. She peered back into the darkness for some sign of the lions but saw nothing.

Grant watched her with undisguised amusement. "I'll get dinner started now," he finally told her, heading into the kitchen.

After one last look for lions, she turned to follow him. "You do your own cooking?"

"Not usually, but Kulu has the night off to be with his family. He does most of the cooking, both here and when we're on safari."

He pulled out a bowl and skillet and some

things from the refrigerator while she watched. "If you're just going to be standing there," he said over his shoulder, "make yourself useful and toss the salad."

There was a bowl of fresh lettuce and tomatoes on the counter. She searched in vain for an apron to put over her skirt. Grant watched her for a moment, then with a wry look, flicked out an extra long dishtowel and tied it around her waist. With his hands on her hips, he turned her around to face him. "Think you can handle it now?"

Alex knew he was teasing her. She had four brothers and she knew teasing. But Grant Adams was *not* her brother, and she found his nearness disconcerting. In self-defense she backed away from him—right into a stepstool sitting innocently behind her.

Grant saw what was happening and caught her before she hit the ground, then set her on her feet, amusement etched in the attractive crinkles at the corners of his brown eyes.

Alex was mortified. She had known the man less than twenty-four hours and had made one stupid, clumsy mistake after another.

"Honestly," she explained lamely, "I'm usually not like this."

He went back to cracking eggs into the bowl. "I'll have to take your word for it."

An offended frown knit her brow. "I see tact isn't one of your strong points."

"If it's tact you want, go to Buckingham Palace. Now toss the salad . . . and try not to get any on the walls."

Dark blue eyes scorched the back of his head, but toss the salad she did. And not a leaf left the bowl. The bracing scent of vinegar mixing with oil put an edge on her already healthy hunger.

He turned two perfectly done cheese omelets onto plates while she served the salad. Then he poured each of them a glass of red wine and they settled at the small, round kitchen table off to one side. He lifted his glass in a brief salute, his eyes on her lovely face, and drank. Alex returned the salute and drank also, holding the smooth, fragrant wine in her mouth a moment before swallowing.

Both ate in silence, and yet each was intensely aware of the other. Grant finished first. He tossed his napkin onto the table next to his plate, then leaned comfortably back in his chair and watched Alex. "What kind of writing do you do?" he finally asked.

She dabbed her mouth thoughtfully and folded her napkin. "Political, mostly."

"Articles or books?"

"Articles, mainly. And one book which sold seven copies. Six to my brothers and parents and one to me."

His smile warmed her. "You have four brothers?"

"Alex nodded ruefully. "All over six feet tall and painfully overprotective of their one sister."

"That's understandable."

She nodded. "You're right. But that doesn't make it any easier to take when you're sixteen. I felt as though I had bodyguards."

"An appropriate word."

She sipped the wine. "I must admit, it was fun growing up in a large family."

He studied her with a quiet intensity. "It sounds as if you're planning a large one of your own."

The warmth of her charmingly shy smile enveloped him. "I'd like that," she admitted.

"What happens if you fall in love with a man who thinks differently?"

She shook her head. "I won't do that."

He raised a sardonic brow. "How can you say that with such certainty?"

"Communication."

"Communication?" he repeated curiously.

"That's right. I'll ask before I fall." She wiggled her brows at him Groucho Marx style, her eyes alight with mischief. "What about you? Do you plan on having lots of children?"

He studied her for a long moment before answering. There was something about her that compelled complete honesty. "Two years ago I was ill. Seriously ill. It left me unable to have children. I'm very lucky that I already had two."

Alex blinked. Of all the responses she had expected, that wasn't one of them. "I'm sorry," she said lamely.

"About what?" he asked wryly. "I'm sterile, not impotent."

Her cheeks pinkened attractively, but she held his gaze. "I'm sorry for flirting with a married man. If I'd known, I wouldn't have."

"A divorced man," he said, correcting her as he wondered at his need to do so. "The boys are visiting their mother for a few weeks."

It didn't occur to her to be surprised at the relief that flooded her system. She didn't want him to be married.

He stood up abruptly and cleared the table while Alex studied his back curiously. His sudden withdrawal was painfully obvious. She would have been a fool not to realize that she had trespassed into some very personal territory.

The screen door in the living room

slammed and a little African boy ran breathlessly into the kitchen, his eyes immediately
finding the doctor. With wild gestures he
described something in Swahili, then at a
sharp command from Grant, ran back out of
the house.

The Australian strode quickly from the
kitchen to his bedroom, Alex on his heels.

"What's going on?' she asked.

He picked up a black medical bag from his
dresser. "A Masai woman is in labor. Has
been for more than twenty-four hours. Apparently something is going wrong and they
don't know what to do to help her."

"Is there anything I can do?"

He looked at her for the first time since his
mention of his divorce. "Have you ever
helped deliver a baby?"

"No. But I'm not squeamish. I can help if
you tell me what to do."

"Come on then." He walked quickly out of
the house and to his Land Rover. "You're all
I've got."

She was less than overwhelmed by his
gratitude but bit back a sarcastic retort.

The Land Rover jolted over the dry riverbed, the light from their headlights bounc-
ing over the landscape until they were up the
bank and on the flat track that led to the
Masai village they had passed through that

morning. He jerked to a stop in front of a small round hut with a thatched roof, much like the one she had sheltered in earlier that evening.

Grant turned sideways, his arm across the back of his seat as he spoke to her. "The mother-to-be is very young. Her husband won't be back for several weeks, and she's frightened. What I want you to do is hold her hand, wipe her forehead, and give her encouragement. Do whatever you think is necessary to help her get through this. The more relaxed you make her, the easier the delivery will be."

"All right." There was no hesitation or dread in her voice, and he found himself suddenly reassessing his initial opinion of her as a spoiled little rich girl.

Without further delay he grabbed his medical bag and walked into the dimly lit hut. There was only one room, sparsely furnished and with a dirt floor. On a small bed off to the side lay the girl, perspiration beading her brow, her enormous brown eyes frightened as they latched onto Alex. A large woman rose from beside the bed and moved to a far corner of the hut. Grant immediately got to work, bathing his hands in alcohol before touching the young woman.

Alex's attention was centered entirely on

the girl. She was lovely. And very, very young. No more than sixteen. "What's her name?" she asked.

"Mary."

She looked at him incredulously. "Mary?"

"Missionary influence."

The girl suddenly had a powerful contraction. "Get her to breathe deeply," ordered Grant. "You'll have to show her. She doesn't speak English."

For the first time, Alex silently thanked her dear friend Kathy for dragging her to natural childbirth classes when Kathy's husband wasn't available. She put her hands on either side of the girl's damp face and forced her to make eye contact, inhaling deeply and exaggeratedly, then parting her lips slightly to exhale. The girl looked at her with a question in her tired eyes, and Alex nodded at her and repeated the procedure. Mary understood and imitated Alex. When the next contraction came, Alex held the girl's face again and forced her to breathe with the pain instead of fighting against it.

"The baby's turned around," Grant said under his breath as he examined her.

Between contractions Alex sat on the edge of the bed and held the girl's hand, smiling at her and speaking soothingly as she wiped the perspiration from Mary's forehead with a cool towel. Grant spoke to the girl in Swahili and she answered rapidly, her face contorting as a contraction began.

"It's coming!" he said in relief. "It won't be long now." And it wasn't. "Short breaths, short breaths," he instructed, and Alex dutifully showed the girl what he meant, keeping one eye on her and the other on his skillful hands as he delivered a very healthy, screaming girl into the world, feet first.

A completely peaceful, amazed, and happy look transformed the Masai girl's face as she took the baby in her arms and held it to her breast.

Grant washed in the alcohol rinse again and dried off with a white towel he carried in his case. Wordlessly he stood behind Alex as she sat on the bed, and then he put his hands on her shoulders. Completely at ease, she relaxed against him with a sigh.

"Welcome to the Serengeti," he said softly.

She tilted her head and smiled up at him tiredly. "I don't think I can take the pace."

He tenderly tucked some heavy strands of hair behind her ear. His thumb brushed her smooth cheek. "You're a surprising woman, Alexandra Hollister."

She closed her eyes and snuggled against him as a slow smile curved her mouth. "Can we go home now?" Her adventures had finally caught up with her.

He liked the easy way she called Banagi

home. Grant signalled to the woman who still stood in a corner of the room and, as she approached, gave her instructions in Swahili on the care of mother and child.

Then he led Alex out into the star-filled African night and helped her into the Land Rover. She sank down on the seat and leaned her head against its back with her eyes closed, enjoying the crisp feel of the air washing over her face as the Land Rover sped through the night to Banagi.

The Australian stopped the Land Rover in front of the house, then lifted Alex out of the passenger seat to carry her in. She wrapped her arms around his neck and laid her head on his shoulder. "I'm not asleep."

"I know," he said quietly as he climbed the veranda steps. The screen door slammed after them. Grant carried her to her room and, holding her with one arm, pulled the covers down with the other and laid her on the bed. When he would have straightened, Alex's grip on his neck tightened and her eyes half-opened. Her mouth curved softly.

Grant disengaged her grasp and leaned over, fully intending to kiss her in brotherly fashion on the forehead, but Alex moved so that his mouth met hers instead. She had no idea why she did it. She surprised herself as much as she had the Australian.

After the initial shock of contact, a slow, steady warmth grew in both of them. He raised his head and gazed into her questioning and confused eyes, then lay down beside her, pulling her pliant body against his taut one. He kissed her tenderly at first, then more deeply as his tongue explored the sweetness of her receptive mouth. His hand slid slowly from her waist to her rounded hip and pulled her even closer against his hard length. There was no question in her mind about his desire.

He pressed her back into the pillow, and his mouth left hers to trail a slow, moist path down her throat while his hand skillfully unbuttoned her blouse and unsnapped her front-fastened silk bra. His tongue sensuously circled her soft, full breast.

Alex gasped. Half of her wanted him to stop. The other half wanted to beg him never to stop. What was happening to her, she wondered? But that was one of her last rational thoughts as her fingers tangled in his thick hair, pressing his face to her more tightly. Waves of indescribable pleasure rolled through her as his mouth traveled over her flat stomach, kissing and tantalizing her.

This is crazy!

A trembling started deep within her. Fear. Desire. She didn't know which.

Grant raised himself above her, a curious frown creasing his forehead. Then realization dawned. He pulled her tenderly into his arms, stroking her silky hair soothingly. "My God," he whispered, "You've never done this before, have you?"

She shook her head.

"You should have said something."

An unsteady smile curved her mouth. "I didn't know how to bring it up."

He pushed the tawny hair away from her damp face and kissed her forehead with a shaky sigh of his own. "How very unfashionable of you."

"Blame my bodyguards."

He got up from the bed and pulled her sheet snugly around a surprised Alex. "One of these days the *right* man is going to thank your bodyguards."

"Grant . . ." Was he simply going to leave things the way they were? What had she done wrong?

No one was more astonished than he at what he was doing. "Alexandra," he said quietly, "I'm not the Prince Charming you've been saving yourself for. Not by a long shot."

She heard the warning in his voice. "I gave up believing in fairy tales when I saw my father's eyes smiling at me from beneath

Santa's bushy brows." Concern was etched in her dark eyes. "I'm not a child, Grant, my inexperience notwithstanding. I'm responsible for my own actions as a woman."

A corner of his mouth lifted. "In this instance, I'm responsible." His brown eyes studied her thoughtfully. "Do you want me to make love to you?"

She met his gaze with a direct one of her own. "I don't know."

A slow smile curved his mouth as he straightened away from her. "Get some sleep. We have a big day ahead of us tomorrow."

He closed the bedroom door behind him and walked onto the veranda. One shoulder leaned against a pillar as he studied the star-studded African skies. Something had become very clear. It would be the easiest thing in the world for him to get involved with her. And it would be disastrous. Alexandra was sensitive and vulnerable, whether she believed it or not. He wouldn't hurt her for the world, and that's exactly what would happen. His sons came first in his life. And that meant a reconciliation with Carolyn to provide them with a normal home—or at least as normal a home as it was possible to have under the circumstances.

Tomorrow he was simply going to have to distance himself from her.

Alexandra lay awake in bed staring at the ceiling long after the Australian had gone. She didn't know what to think. But one thing was clear to her. He hadn't rejected her as a person. He actually thought he was being noble. And perhaps he was, after all.

She rolled onto her side and hugged a pillow tightly against her. Grant was a man with things on his mind and deeds to accomplish. He viewed her as an interference—and he might just be right. All she knew was that Grant Adams was a special man and that he was destined to play a special part in her life. She knew that as well as she knew her name.

But she explored no deeper. Sleep came quietly, overtaking her. She had had quite a day.

Chapter Three

When Alex awoke the next morning it took her a moment to get her bearings. And once she remembered she was at Banagi, she also remembered the night before.

A smile curved her mouth. She wasn't embarrassed. There was no hesitation in her heart about facing Grant today. What had happened between them, though it wasn't much, had felt *right*. She couldn't be in love with him. And she wasn't going to kid herself into thinking he felt anything other than attraction for her. But there was nothing wrong with that.

Even as she was thinking these things, she was amazed at herself. Was this the same woman who had left the United States three days earlier? It hardly seemed possible. How could anyone's outlook change so much in such a short time?

She would have been wise to search her heart for the answer, but she didn't. Sounds of men talking on the veranda forced her from the comfort of her bed. It was undoubtedly time to leave for the poacher's camp.

She dressed in slim-fitting jeans and a tailored short-sleeved shirt, then packed some clothes in a flight bag for the overnight safari.

Jundi was on the veranda with several uniformed African rangers. They were going over a map tacked on the outside wall. Jundi stopped talking to greet her politely and introduce her to the other men, who shyly shook her hand. He went back over the route for her benefit, showing her exactly where they intended to drive that day and camp for the night.

Her eyes followed his finger on the map. "How long will it take to get there?"

"Several hours over rough terrain. But that is the easy part. Once there we must hack our way into the bush with machetes."

The screen door creaked and slammed. Grant, his hair still damp from the shower, stood there with a stern look as he rolled his shirt-sleeves halfway up his powerful forearms. His eyes touched on Alex, but there was no acknowledgement in them. Her smile faded and her gaze dropped. Suddenly, she was embarrassed. She might not regret what had happened, but he obviously did. It hurt.

"Is everyone ready?" He spoke to Jundi.

The African in turn checked with Alex. "Miss?"

"I just need to get my camera equipment. It's in my room." She sprinted into the house and gathered her equipment. Then, after she had rummaged through her flight bag to make sure she had enough film to carry her through the trip, she raced back out. She came to a full stop on the top veranda step and looked around in surprise. Everyone was gone. Everyone except Jundi, who was waiting in a Land Rover with the engine running. He signalled for her to hurry. She sprang down the steps and quickly climbed in. Jundi took off immediately, throwing her back against the seat.

"Where did everyone go?" She tried not to sound as bewildered as she felt.

"The doctor is in a hurry today. He went ahead with the others and asked me to bring you."

Jundi accelerated even more, forcing Alex to hold the sides of her seat to keep from being bounced around.

The African flashed her a friendly smile. "Have no worry, Miss. I will get you there in one piece."

Her grip loosened a little. This was her second snub from the Australian. There was no reason why he couldn't have waited five minutes for her if he'd wanted to. Obviously he hadn't.

Alex deliberately pushed him from her mind. "How long have you been a ranger?" she shouted over the hard-working engine.

"Many years," he yelled back. "Many!"

"How long have you worked with the doctor?"

"Five years—as long as he's been here."

She couldn't resist. "What sort of man do you find him to be?"

Jundi glanced at her sideways. "You are very curious about our doctor."

"Guilty," she admitted.

His eyes returned to the plain. "He is a good man. And a very unhappy one."

"Unhappy," she said thoughtfully. "Why?"

He smiled at her persistence. "If he wishes you to know his life story, he will tell you himself. It is not my place to do so."

Her cheeks pinkened slightly. "I'm sorry, Jundi. It wasn't my intention to put you in an awkward position."

He pointed suddenly. "There! There are the others."

Her gaze followed his finger. The Land Rovers, four abreast, swept across the sunlit plain leaving jet streams of dust in their wake. When Jundi caught up they were five abreast. It was a stunning sight, and despite some bone-jarring encounters with her seat, Alex was exhilarated. She felt alive with the wind whipping her hair about and the sun hot on her body. She found Grant's sun-bleached head in the Land Rover furthest away and slightly ahead of the others.

When the terrain smoothed out Jundi handed her his field glasses. Carefully she stood on her seat, elbows resting on the edge of the windshield, and looked out over the plain. Impala loped gracefully, scattering at the noisy approach of the vehicles. A giraffe nibbled the upper branches of a flat-topped tree; then, frightened by the Land Rovers, galloped away in slow motion, his long neck stretching elegantly with each stride.

They drove to the edge of the plain, then headed into the bush. Grant stopped at the place he thought could be penetrated most easily with machetes, and the others came to a halt beside him.

Alex climbed out of the Land Rover and began snapping pictures. She forced herself not to search for Grant. If he wanted to act as though nothing had happened between them that was fine with her.

She got a few more pictures as the men hacked at the brush and vines, their shining machetes reflecting the sun. One man started a Swahili song and the others soon joined in, their words punctuated by the rhythmic swish of the blades.

"Alexandra."

She looked up, startled, into the Australian's unsmiling eyes.

He handed her a machete. "You can start next to Jundi."

She looked from the blade to the man. "You can't be serious. I don't know how to handle one of these things."

"You'll be amazed how quickly you learn as you go along."

"But that's ridiculous. I just came along to take pictures."

"Are you saying you don't want to carry your own weight?"

The words "I can handle anything you can throw at me" returned to haunt her. Eyes narrowed expressively, she put her camera on the seat of the Land Rover with more force than was strictly necessary and lugged the heavy machete to the designated spot. She watched Jundi closely before attempting to use it herself. Hacking through brush was terrifically demanding work. Her muscles were going to ache for days, but she kept at it, although she was not nearly as efficient as the rangers, or Grant himself for that matter. She did the best she could, and pride kept her going. Perspiration soaked her blouse and dripped from the tip of her nose.

She took a breather, leaning tiredly on the handle of the machete. Grant was working three men down, his back to her. A corner of her mind noticed that he was left-handed. The rest of her mind noticed the muscles in his back and shoulders rippling under the bronzed skin, glistening in the heat as though oiled. His shirt lay discarded on the ground some ten feet away. The veins on his biceps and forearms were raised from the tremendous amount of force he was exerting.

She had to drag her eyes away from him. Why did he have to be so damned attractive, she wondered as she got back to work.

It took them hours, but they finally broke through the thick mess into a clearing. Grant carelessly toweled the perspiration from his torso and threw on his shirt as he spoke with the men in their language. Then he turned to Alex. "I think you should wait here."

She eyed him incredulously. "I help you hack your way through this and then you tell me you think I should wait here? I think not, Doctor."

"It could be dangerous."

"How so?"

He ran his hand through his hair more in frustration than anything else; he was unused to having to answer to anyone. "If there are poachers still in there, they aren't going to be happy to see us. They've been known to get violent when crossed. And we also don't know what animals are in there. This isn't a game, Alexandra."

"I didn't for a minute suppose it was," she retorted. Then was immediately annoyed with herself. "I'm sorry," she said apologetically, rubbing her hot forehead. "I didn't mean to sound like a shrew." Her eyes met his. "It's just that I think I should be part of the whole experience, taking pictures with my mind as well as my camera. Granted," she added wryly, "I hadn't planned on hacking my way through brush, but I'm glad I did now that it's over."

A muscle in his cheek moved. "Suit yourself," he said abruptly and walked away from her into the clearing.

Alex breathed deeply and counted to ten before following. One of these days he was going to push her temper over the edge, and then . . . look out, Dr. Grant Adams.

There was a small dry riverbed that they followed on foot for over a mile to yet another cleared area and a shallow pool of water. Grant suddenly stopped, completely alert. "They've been here," he finally said, breaking the somehow terrible silence.

Everything seemed normal to Alex. "How do you know?"

"This is the only water for miles. It should be surrounded by wildlife and it isn't."

"What do we do now?" Her voice dropped to a whisper.

"You stay here." Then he gave the men their orders in Swahili and they split into two groups.

It happened so quickly that she automatically obeyed—until everyone was out of sight and she realized that she was completely alone. She was very frightened as she stood exposed in the still clearing.

A twig snapped behind her and she jumped, her hand over her heart. But nothing was there. The decision to disobey Grant was the easiest one she'd ever made. She struck out on her own in the direction in which he and his men had gone.

Finding them turned out to be more difficult than she'd imagined. There were no familiar landmarks. No footprints in the dry earth. No voices. Nothing. She had to force herself to remain calm, knowing that there was a very good possibility she was lost. She tried to find her way back to the dry riverbed, but it was hopeless. It had to be near, but where?

It was with a great sigh of relief that she spotted a clearing and headed for it, assuming it was the riverbed. But when she got there she found it was a camp. She stopped quite a distance away and looked for signs of life, but there were none. She cautiously walked toward it then stopped, appalled. Nothing in her life had prepared her for what she found. In numbed horror she looked around the heart of the camp. Rack upon rack of drying meat and animal skins were piled high. Two zebra and a once beautiful gazelle lay dead, thrown in a heap as carelessly as somebody's trash. There was a rare rhinoceros, butchered only for his horn. The smell of death lay heavy in the air.

The carnage was terrible, unlike anything Alex had imagined. She was sickened but helpless to turn away.

Suddenly Grant was beside her, swearing softly under his breath at her disobedience. He turned her into his arms and pressed her face into his shoulder. Her fingers dug into his arms, but her eyes were wide open and dry.

"Poachers?" she asked hoarsely, looking up at him.

His jaw was taut. "Yes."

"But why?"

"The best reason of all for some people. Money."

She leaned her forehead against his shoulder. "My God."

He held her quietly, his chin resting on the top of her head while he looked around, his eyes black with anger. "I'll have Jundi walk you back to the cars."

She took a strengthening breath and pushed herself away from him. "No. I can handle it. Pictures should be taken. People have to see what's happening."

"I'll take them." He didn't want her exposed to this nightmare. The reason he had left her in the clearing in the first place was to protect her.

His obvious concern touched her. "Thank you. But this is something I have to do myself."

And she did. It was the most difficult thing she had ever undertaken, but while the men collected a mountain of hideous traps and carefully began burning the camp, she photographed it all.

The Australian watched her with increasing admiration. She was stubborn, but she had courage. Perhaps he had been hasty in writing Banagi off.

Darkness had fallen by the time they got back to the Land Rovers and got camp set up. Alex assembled her own tent with the ease of experience, then washed thoroughly in bottled water and changed into a comfortable blue cotton skirt and long-sleeved blouse.

Stepping out of her tent, she saw the others gathered around a pleasant fire. Grant was with them, speaking in Swahili, making the men laugh.

Alex stood motionless and quietly watched, not wanting to draw attention to herself. It was nice to see them happy, but she couldn't join in. The sights in the poachers' camp weighed heavily on her.

Grant spotted her in the darkness and his smile slowly faded. He knew exactly how she felt. He had been there himself many times. It still affected him, but never as badly as the first time.

He left the fire and walked to her. Alex stood unmoving, watching as he approached. He stopped before her, his dark eyes surprisingly sympathetic. "Would you like to walk before dinner?"

There was no hesitation. "I would, yes."

Grant directed her away from the camp with a hand in the middle of her back. "Want to talk about it?" he asked as they walked.

A sad smile lifted the corners of her mouth. "I don't know what to say other than the obvious. I can't get it out of my mind.

Even when I close my eyes it's there, behind my lids." She stopped walking and faced him, though his face was hidden in the night shadows from her probing gaze. "How did you get over your first poaching camp?"

"Time. I've never been angrier in my life. It fired my determination to rid this land of all the bastards who kill as easily as breathing, without any thought of the suffering they cause. And all for the almighty dollar."

They continued their walk, each wrapped in his own thoughts. "Did they know we were coming?" she asked.

"They must have. It's the only reason they would have cleared out so quickly and so inefficiently."

"Was it Kabloona?"

His smile touched her through the night. "What do you know about him?"

"Nothing. I heard you mention his name once as a poacher."

They turned back to camp. "No. Kabloona is more humane than the group we raided today. At least when he kills he does it quickly and painlessly."

There was something in his voice. Alex glanced up at him. "You like him, don't you?"

He paused. "Yes. I suppose I do. He's a well-educated man, much like Jundi. He doesn't massacre entire herds but takes only what he needs to support himself and his huge following in the style to which they've become accustomed."

"If he's well educated, can't you reason with him?"

"I've tried, believe me. I don't want to send him to prison. But it's no use. Poaching is a family business and has been for generations."

"Is he Masai?"

"No way. The Masai wouldn't dream of poaching. They're herdsmen. In the four hundred years they've lived on the Serengeti, they've protected it as best they could against other tribes who didn't respect the land and its inhabitants. Jundi is a Masai, as are the other rangers out here tonight."

"But they've obviously broken away from the African tribal mold."

"They've all been to the city. And they returned to the Serengeti more sophisticated but still respecting the rites and traditions of their tribe. Most of the men are married to native Masai women and live with them in the village."

"Does the village have a school?"

"It used to have a missionary school, but that closed nearly a decade ago. Since then, nothing."

"That's tragic." She thought of the baby delivered only last night and wondered what kind of future she would have, uneducated in a hostile world.

The campfire flickered ahead, beckoning. Grant looked down at the woman by his side. "Feel better?"

"A little," she answered quietly. "Thank you."

"Hungry?"

"Always!"

Kulu had set up a kitchen with another fire outside the camp. Grant took Alex there and filled a plate for her, then helped himself. Together they walked to the fire and sat with the others.

She really did feel better, she thought as she sat cross-legged on the hard ground, balancing the serviceable metal plate on one knee. Grant's kindness and consideration had helped her. But the wall he had built between them after last night was still there.

The tinny scraping of utensils against plates filled the night as the men ate and talked. Grant spoke seriously with Jundi. Alex's thoughts drifted to her article as she ate. Her idea in the hut the night before of keeping a journal and using it as the basis for her work became more appealing with every hour. So much had happened already that filling a magazine after a four-week visit should be a simple task.

Her eyes touched on the Australian and

stayed there. The interesting contours of his face were highlighted by the campfire. He used his hands to make a point, and she found herself watching the long fingers and remembering how they had felt on her body last night. . . .

She dragged her eyes away, surprised at herself. As far as he was concerned, nothing had happened between them. He had made that abundantly clear. If his coolness was because he feared clinging women, he had nothing to dread from her.

She rose abruptly and took her plate to Kulu. Then, excusing herself politely to the group in general, and pointedly to no one in particular, she went to her tent, curled up on the cot with a note pad, and began her journal.

The minutes flew by as she wrote, engrossed. Vaguely she heard the sounds of the camp settling into sleep. When her own eyes grew heavy, she put her things on a table beside the cot and undressed in the light of the hurricane lantern.

Grant was the only one left by the smoldering fire. He stretched his legs out before him as he leaned on an elbow. His eyes narrowed on Alex's tent. Her body was clearly outlined against the canvas as she stood in front of her lamp undressing.

With exquisite grace she slid her arms

from her blouse. The skirt dropped around her ankles and she bent to retrieve it, folding it neatly and packing it. She picked up what he presumed to be a bottle of body lotion and began stroking it into her skin, tilting her head back and smoothing it onto her arched throat, then following the line of her body, massaging it into her breasts and flat stomach and in long, slow strokes up her shapely legs. He found himself imagining that those were his hands trailing over that soft skin. . . . Still a nude silhouette, Alex brushed her shining hair in slow motion.

The man couldn't take his eyes off her. It was one of the most provocative, enticing displays he had ever witnessed—more so because he knew she was completely unaware of being watched. He was aroused. Hungry for her. He wanted to take her in his arms and kiss her into passionate incoherency.

She pulled a prim short nightgown over her head. He watched enviously as it flowed over her body to just above her knees. Some nightgowns had all the luck. With a final stretch, she sat on the cot and turned off the lamp.

The Australian fell back onto the grass with a groan and stared up at the sky. His body needed time to recover.

What was it about *this* woman, this Alexandra Hollister, that wouldn't allow him to put her out of his mind? She had haunted his dreams last night and she would probably haunt them again tonight. And not only for the obvious reasons. She had been here such a short time, yet he was finding that he enjoyed being with her. She was bright and funny and sensitive. And just clumsy enough to be enchanting. There was an innate warmth that radiated from her, a goodness, that drew him.

Oh yes, there was more to his feelings for her than simple desire. He liked her.

He turned his eyes toward the darkened tent. He had hurt her this morning. That had been his intention, and it had been done to protect himself. But now it was becoming equally important to him that she be protected. Protected from him as much as anything. In some insane way he felt responsible for her.

But he wasn't.

He turned his head away from Alex's tent once more, as though by that simple gesture he could sever their invisible bond.

Chapter Four

Camp sounds woke Alex the next morning. After a quick splash of water and brush of teeth, she put on navy blue shorts and a bright white shirt-front sweatshirt with blue on the yoke and around the front snaps. After packing her things, she dismantled her tent and was ready to go. The others were in the process of doing the same. She lifted her paraphernalia into the back of Jundi's Land Rover then sat on the passenger seat waiting for everyone else to finish.

"Good morning."

Her heart skipped a beat at the sound of Grant's voice so near. She looked up at him, her hand shading her eyes from the stark sun. "Good morning."

"Aren't you having breakfast?"

"I don't like food in the morning."

"You Americans have bad eating habits."

"And yet we live longer than any other people on earth. Curious, isn't it?"

A corner of his mouth lifted. "You're very alert, considering the hour."

"Thank you, I think."

"You're welcome. I also wanted to tell you that I think you handled yourself well yesterday. I have only one suggestion."

She lifted a questioning brow.

"When you undress in a tent at night, don't stand in front of the lantern."

Her eyes grew wide.

"Not that I objected, mind you. On the contrary. I was mesmerized."

Annoyance flashed from dark blue depths. "A decent man would have looked the other way."

"I never claimed to be decent. Remember that well, Alexandra."

Her lips parted in astonishment as she watched him walk away. That man was beginning to rile her, and he'd better watch his step. When you had to defend yourself against four brothers, you learned how to handle anything and anyone.

* * *

After an uneventful day that turned up no new poaching camps, they returned to Banagi. She traveled with Jundi once more. The longer they were together, the more she liked him. *He* was a decent man.

Grant gave Kulu the night off again to be with his family since he had been away from them the night before.

Alex cleaned up and changed into sea-green slacks and a white shirt with just a hint of the same green in the thin stripes running through it. She pushed her hair away from her face with a narrow matching plastic headband, then sat on the veranda swing, moving gently to and fro as she added to her journal, stopping occasionally to nibble thoughtfully on the end of her pen.

She had been sitting there for only a short time when Grant came out through the squeaking screen door. He had changed also, into natural-colored slacks and a V-necked summer sweater with the sleeves pushed casually up his forearms. She caught a tantalizing hint of his aftershave lotion.

"Do you want a drink?" he asked.

"Wine would be nice."

He disappeared into the house again and returned a few minutes later with two glasses. After handing her one he sat on the top step and leaned his back against the railing. He drew one knee up and rested the hand holding the wine along it while he looked out over the moonlit plain. Occasional flashes of silent lightning rent the clear sky, a sign of an electrical storm hundreds of miles away. The night was pleasantly breezeless—a perfect evening for writing, but the presence of the Australian threw her concentration off. She couldn't stop looking at him, though he hadn't acknowledged her presence since bringing her the wine. He was in a place away where she couldn't reach him.

"A nickel for your thoughts," she finally said softly.

He glanced at her. "A nickel?"

"Inflation."

The grooves in his cheeks deepened and his gaze returned to the plain. "They're private, Alexandra."

"You're a very private person."

"That's right."

She gave up that tactic. He obviously had no intention of telling her. "Why do you call me Alexandra rather than Alex?"

Brown eyes touched her and roamed leisurely over her slimly rounded figure. "You look like an Alexandra to me. Alex is boyish. You're not."

"I was on an all-boy little league baseball team before it was fashionable."

A smile lit his eyes. "I'll bet you were."

"I'm great at touch football and tennis."

"We'll have to play sometime."

She paused. "If you'd like me to shut up, say so."

He leaned the back of his head against the railing. "Don't. I get tired of being alone with my thoughts."

She studied him intently. "You know, Grant, if you ever *do* feel like talking to someone, I'm a good listener. I've even been known to give good advice on occasion . . . at least I'm still on speaking terms with most of my friends."

"Only most?"

She shrugged. "Everybody screws up once in awhile."

Grant's laugh filled the night and sent a shiver of pleasure down her spine.

A comfortable silence fell between them. Alex went back to her writing, unaware of the Australian's eyes on her downturned face, watching every nuance of expression that crossed it. "What's it like growing up in a large family?" he asked suddenly.

She looked up, surprised by the odd question. "I don't know how to answer that. Fun would be a good word, I suppose. There was always someone to talk to or fight with. We had some great backyard soccer matches." She smiled. "There was—and is—lots of love."

"Are your parents divorced?"

She smiled, thinking of the smooching that still went on. "No way. Still married and still mad about each other."

"So your family is close."

"Very. My brothers and I have all settled within easy driving distance of our folks." She scribbled a design on her writing pad. "You'd like my family."

He didn't say anything.

"What's it like growing up an only child?" she asked in a challenging tone.

He shrugged. "I suppose it depends on the kind of parents you have. Mine were never there. I was raised by a succession of nurses and nannies. In a word, I was lonely," he said thoughtfully. "I walked through my childhood wondering what was wrong with me, because my parents didn't really seem to care that I existed. And as I got older and into my teens, that insecurity got worse."

Her heart went out to the little boy he had been. "You don't seem insecure now."

"I'm not. I know my worth as a human being. But it took a long time."

"Where are your parents now?"

"Dead." He rose abruptly, unwilling to talk about it anymore. "Hungry?"

"A little."

"Is a ham sandwich all right?"

"That's fine." She set her pad on the seat next to her so she could help, but he put his hands on her shoulders to hold her in place. "Stay out here and enjoy the night," he told her. "I'm capable of making two sandwiches alone."

The screen door slammed after him. Alex frowned but stayed where she was. The wall between them had come down for a few precious seconds, but he had erected it again immediately.

With a sigh she sank down on the swing and gazed up at the sky. She pushed with her feet to set it in motion. It didn't creak as she had expected it to do but moved silently in the still night.

Alex felt that there was no place on earth quite like Banagi. Her understanding of what the Australian was attempting to accomplish and why grew with every hour. If he didn't succeed, all of this would eventually be gone.

A shooting star caught her eye. She stopped the swing and moved to the edge of the porch to watch as it streaked across the sky into oblivion, then closed her eyes and made a wish.

Grant returned with two plates and handed her one before sitting on the steps with his. Alex sat next to him. "I think you'll be getting all the money you need to run Banagi," she told him, just before biting into the sandwich.

He glanced at her in surprise. "Why?"

She looked back at the sky with a little smile. "Let's just say that I've yet to meet a shooting star able to refuse my requests."

"Your scientific approach leaves me speechless with admiration."

Alex wagged a friendly finger. "You'll live to regret your skepticism."

Grant raised his wineglass to her in a brief salute. "To regrets."

Her wineglass was near the swing, so she settled for inclining her head. "Regrets."

They finished the meal in silence. Sitting with him on the steps had been a mistake. He filled her senses. She liked the look of him, the feel of him, the scent of him. She couldn't get their night together out of her mind, though he seemed to have forgotten it completely.

Their knees were not quite touching. If she moved hers just a little to the right . . . How ridiculous! What had gotten into her? She was thinking like a child instead of a woman. And she felt so much like a woman when he was near.

She rose abruptly. "If you'll excuse me, I think I'll go to bed. Uh, to sleep."

"It's early." He rose also.

She shook her head as she walked away from him. "I'm beginning to feel that it's later than we think," she muttered.

In her room she closed the door and took a deep, much-needed breath before undressing and pulling a numbered football jersey over her head. After snapping out the light, she climbed between crisp, clean sheets and burrowed into her pillow.

Her eyes flew open suddenly when her foot touched something cold, dry, and reptilian. It moved and she screamed, but she stayed in the bed, terrified that if it was a snake it would attack if she got so much as a nervous tic.

Her bedroom door crashed open and the Australian stood there, framed by the light behind him. "What the hell . . . !"

"There's a snake in my bed." Fear made her voice husky.

He turned on the light and came near her. "Are you all right?"

"Just get it out of here!"

It moved against her foot again, but this time it was more than she could stand. With another scream she leaped out of bed and behind Grant flinging her arms around his waist. She could handle anything but snakes. That was too much to ask, even of Alex.

She felt Grant's body shake, but when she realized he was laughing, her arms dropped and she came curiously out from behind. "What's so funny?"

He inclined his head toward a frog sitting calmly on the floor. "There's your snake."

Alex closed her eyes, a chagrined smile on her lovely face. "This is really embarrassing."

Still laughing, he pulled her into his arms and stroked her hair. It felt good to be there, and she relaxed against him.

Grant's smile faded as the warmth of her body seeped through his clothes and into him. It seemed so right.

Alex felt his heartbeat accelerate. She also felt his sudden withdrawal, though he didn't move.

She stepped away from him, her eyes downcast. "Thank you for coming to my rescue. I think I'll try to get some sleep now."

He started away from her but turned back and took her chin in a gentle hand, raising her face to his while stroking her smooth cheek with his thumb. "I want you, you know."

Her eyes touched his. "I know."

He quietly closed the door behind him and left Alex alone once more.

She turned out the light and lay on the bed, her hands behind her head, staring at the blank ceiling. She seemed to be doing a lot of that lately. But then she couldn't remember ever being more confused than she was now. There was something between them. But was it anything worth discovering? Particularly when he seemed so anxious *not* to?

Hours later something disturbed her sleep. She lay in the dark, her eyes suddenly open, wide awake. There had been no noise. Just a presence.

Rolling onto her back, she gasped at the sight of an African standing silently next to her bed staring down at her, a spear in one hand. Instinctively she pulled the covers up to her chin. "Who are you? What do you want?" She was more annoyed than afraid.

"You come with me."

"I most certainly will not."

"Kabloona wants to see you."

"Then tell Mr. Kabloona to come here."

She pulled the sheet from the mattress and wrapped it around her, then got out of bed and padded to the door, bent on getting Grant to handle this. The African caught her arm and stopped her. "The doctor is not here."

She shook his hand off. "Of course he is. It must be three o'clock in the morning." But he wasn't. She walked across the hall unhindered by the African and looked into his room. It was deserted, the bed not slept in. Her heart sank. What was she supposed to do?

The African was right behind her. "Now you come with me. Kabloona won't hurt you. He only wants to talk; he knows you are a writer, and he wants to tell his side of the story."

If his intention had been to pique her interest, he had succeeded. "You mean you'll take me to his camp?"

"Yes. He will talk to you there."

"It would make a wonderful twist to the story," she said thoughtfully, more to herself than to her companion. She glanced down at her football jersey and sheet. "All right. I'll go. But I can't very well go dressed like this. Let me change and leave a note for Grant . . ."

"You dress, but no note. He will know where you are."

"But . . ."

"Please. We must hurry."

Alex rummaged through her things for jeans and a shirt, leaving drawers opened and clothing discarded on the sheetless bed in her haste. She grabbed a large shoulder bag, her pad, and some pens and camera equipment, then met the African in the living room. "I'm ready."

He inclined his head and Alex followed him out through the front door and down the veranda steps. He stopped suddenly and hurled his spear into the ground. "Now the doctor will know where you are," he told his surprised companion, then walked down the incline and across the riverbed.

Alex followed, a little more nervous than she cared to admit but game nonetheless for the adventure that was sure to follow. She didn't believe for a second that she was in danger. Kabloona might be a poacher, but according to Grant, he was also a gentleman.

They walked for hours, mostly in silence. Early in the journey she had expected to find a Land Rover secreted in the trees, but no such luck. The sun rose and the temperature with it. The back of her neck grew damp and her hair clung hotly to it. The African seemed unperturbed by the heat and completely tireless.

It was noon before they finally came to a secluded area of the bush where a barely noticeable path had been hacked out for pedestrians. They made their way to a clearing and "civilization." Tents filled the camp. Again she saw racks of drying meat, but there was no evidence of the brutality of the other poachers.

Her companion left her as a tall man dressed in khaki bermuda shorts and a neat matching shirt exited the largest tent to greet her. He took her hand in his and smiled down at her. "Good day, Miss Hollister. I am pleased that you were able to join us today."

She guessed his age at about thirty, though it was difficult to tell. His skin was as dark as the night sky. She liked him.

"You must be Kabloona."

He inclined his head. "I am, indeed."

"How did you find out who I was and why I'm here?" she asked curiously.

"Ah, the Serengeti has an amazing grapevine, you will find. There is very little that goes on that everyone here does not know about." He motioned toward his tent. "Please, Miss Hollister, you must be hungry after your journey. Join me for lunch."

Kabloona held the flap for her so she could duck inside. The tent was surprisingly well furnished and comfortable. On a table next to his bed were books in English. Alex and her host sat on a colorful mat while a woman brought them bowls of food. She glanced shyly at Alex and smiled, then wordlessly left them alone. "Is that your wife?" Alex asked curiously.

"One of them."

She looked at him in surprise. "How many do you have?"

"Three."

She tasted the delicate meat set before her and found it delicious. "What is this?" Then she suddenly held up her hand. "No, wait. Don't tell me until later."

He inclined his head. "As you wish. I will, however, share with you that it is not one of the so-called endangered species the doctor is so intent upon saving."

"His endangered species are not 'so-called,' Mr. Kabloona. There is a very real problem with their declining numbers."

"True," he agreed. "And he is helping their numbers when he shuts down poaching operations. I applaud his efforts."

Alex found that incongruous. "And yet you yourself are a poacher."

"With a difference. I poach very little for profit. Mostly it is to feed my people. This is the way we have done things for centuries. These animals belong to us."

"Surely there must be another way. Couldn't you herd, as the Masai do?"

"Never. It is not our way."

"But things change. Perhaps your people could as well."

The African smiled at her. "I see the doctor has converted you to his way of thinking already."

"He has," she said firmly. "With the help of a poachers' camp I saw yesterday."

"Undoubtedly run by profiteers," he said disgustedly.

"Undoubtedly," she agreed.

They ate in silence, each taking the measure of the other. After lunch, they spent the afternoon wandering around Kabloona's camp, examining the kinds of traps he used and discussing his philosophy of life in the bush. He resented being told by outsiders what he and his people could and could not hunt, and when and where. He honestly believed that the animals of the Serengeti belonged to the hunters. Not to the mass murderers who killed for money but to the tribesmen who needed to hunt to survive. While Alex agreed with him in principle, she made an effort to point out that whether they liked it or not, the butchers existed, and for the sake of the wildlife they had to be stopped. And in areas where certain species were becoming rare, the laws had to include everyone, even those who killed to eat.

She met his other wives and many of his children, and learned that he ran his camp with an iron hand. Her respect for the man grew by the hour. Unfortunately, he would not allow pictures, so her camera remained unused in her purse.

At the end of the tour Kabloona helped her into an old Land Rover, much to her relief, and the same young man who had walked her to the camp now sat in the driver's seat. Kabloona took her hand in his and held it for a long moment. "I like you, Miss," he told her. "And I have much admiration for your Doctor Adams. Please, tell him for me that I am not the enemy. I wish to take only what is rightfully mine and my people's. And if I find those who abuse the land or the wildlife, I will get word to him about where to find them. We wish only to live peacefully, in our own way."

"I'll tell him."

He inclined his head toward the driver and off they went. It was late in the evening when he finally stopped and handed her a flashlight. "You get out here and walk the rest of the way."

She looked into the darkness. "I couldn't possibly," she informed him. "There's no way I could find my way back to Banagi."

"And I will go no closer. Searchers will be out. If I am caught, I will be arrested. You must go alone."

"But . . ."

"Follow the track. It will take you there."

She turned on the flashlight, and for the first time realized that he had taken her to the same track she had driven over on her arrival. It certainly wasn't the way they had walked last night.

She stepped out of the Land Rover, confident that she could find her way now. Before she could say thank you to the African, he sped off into the night, leaving her alone.

She stood there for a moment, uneasy about her vulnerability in the open like this, but straightened her shoulders and started on the journey to Banagi.

It turned out to be a good three-hour walk, and she had walked for seven hours that morning. The night noises were frightening, but she kept going until she saw the welcome lights of Banagi. Her walk turned into a run for the last quarter of a mile, until she was safely up the steps and inside the house.

"Grant?" she called breathlessly. "I'm back!" Alex walked through the house, but there was no sign of him.

She sank onto the couch in disappointment and exhaustion, kicking her shoes off and massaging her aching feet. Leaning her head against the back of the couch, she closed her eyes with a sigh. What a day.

The screen door crashed open, startling her and bringing her to her feet. Grant stood in front of her, his brown eyes furious. His hands dug into her shoulders as he shook her. "Don't you *ever* do that to me again, do you understand?"

"Grant . . ." she tried to explain, stunned by his anger.

He took several deep breaths. "Do you have any idea how many man-hours have been wasted today, while we were looking for you?"

"But the spear—didn't you know I was with Kabloona?"

He let go of her and ran his hand distractedly through his hair. "I knew who you were with, but I didn't know where. I didn't know if you were all right or if Kabloona intended to use you to bargain with me." He turned his eyes on her again. "I was frantic."

With a groan that told her he was as angry with himself as he was with her, he pulled her into his arms and held her close, his face buried in her fragrant hair. "God, Alexandra, what are you doing to me?"

He crushed her mouth beneath his, but as he felt her lips softly part to receive him, tenderness welled in him and his kiss grew gentle and exploring. Her arms went around his neck and his around her slender body, pulling her against him and holding her there, as though he couldn't get close enough. He kissed his slow way across her cheek to her ear, kissing the lobe and all around it and down the back of her neck, sending a shiver of delight down her spine. He inhaled sharply when she arched against him.

Quickly, he lifted her in his arms and carried her to the bedroom. He set her on her feet in front of him and began unbuttoning her blouse. His mouth trailed down her throat, kissing above each button he undid until he was finished. Then he ran his hands under the blouse, caressing her shoulders and sliding the blouse off.

Alex took her cue from him and unbuttoned his shirt as her mouth moved with slow sensuality over his smooth, bronzed shoulder and down his muscled chest. She savored the fresh scent and salty taste of his skin.

With slow deliberation, he lowered her onto the bed and covered her body with his own as they kissed once more. Both of them were beyond rational thought. All they wanted was to quench the fires that raged, to fulfill a need so great it was almost painful.

"Doctor?"

At first neither of them heard the voice coming from the living room.

"Doctor?" It was Jundi. Grant lifted himself above Alex with a groan. She wrapped her arms around his neck and held him there.

"Ssshhh," she whispered. "Maybe if we're quiet he'll go away."

He wasn't about to argue as his mouth came down on hers and passionately plundered it.

But Jundi didn't give up. Grant finally rolled off her onto his back and covered his eyes with his forearm while he gave his body a chance to recover before finding out what was going on. Alex felt as though every nerve in her body were coiled.

He got up from the bed and put his shirt on, looking regretfully at Alex's flushed cheeks and passion-glazed eyes. He shook his head with a sigh. "This had better be important."

She heard them talking in the living room in low voices. Then Grant came back to the bedroom. "I have to go to the village. Someone is sick."

She sat up and hugged her knees to herself. "Can I help?"

He trailed the back of his hand down her cheek. "Not this time."

He turned away, but Alex's voice stopped him. "I think I could fall in love with you, Grant Adams."

He turned back to her, his brown eyes serious. "Don't. It wouldn't work. It couldn't."

He left and Alex rested her chin on her

bent knees. A solitary tear spilled from the corner of her eye and fell onto her leg. She had a lot of things to sort out.

The Australian stood on the porch for a moment before heading for the village, staring unseeingly into the night. What was happening to his life? He had had things so well mapped out for his future, including remarriage to his ex-wife. But, because of Alexandra Hollister, a woman who should have been poison to him from their first meeting, things were less clear all the time. It had taken the scare of losing her for all those hours to bring home the realization that what he felt for her wasn't casual.

He tiredly rubbed his forehead and sighed. Things were just going to have to work themselves out, because he sure as hell didn't know what to do.

Chapter Five

When Alex stepped outside the next morning, she found a tall, doe-eyed African woman sitting on the veranda steps. She rose at Alex's approach and smiled shyly.

"How do you do, Miss Hollister," she said softly in the beautiful English Alex was becoming accustomed to hearing.

Alex returned her smile. "I'm fine, thank you." She looked at the young woman curiously. "Have we met?"

"Oh, no, but you know my husband, Jundi. I am Keasa."

"Well, hello. You're exactly the way I had pictured you." She smiled again. "Are you looking for him?" Alex's eyes traveled over the compound and found no sign of human occupation. "I don't know where everyone went."

Keasa sat back down on the step and Alex joined her. "I know where they are. The doctor asked me to stay here with you until his return."

"I don't understand . . ."

"I think he wanted to make sure you wouldn't wander off."

That certainly put Alex in her place.

The two women sat in silence. The hot day was surprisingly still. Very little noise. No breeze. An insect buzzed by Alex's ear, and she waved it away.

Heat covered the plain and rose in waves, blurring the horizon. What animals she could see sought shelter under the few flat-topped trees dotting the vastness.

Alex glanced at the African woman. "You know, Keasa, you really don't have to stay here. I won't leave."

She shook her head. "I gave my word to the doctor."

Alex sighed. "Well, did he say we couldn't go anywhere together?"

"No. Where would you wish to go?"

"The Masai village. I'd like to meet the people—check on the baby I helped deliver my first night here."

"I see no problem with that."

Alex went back into the house and got her shoulder bag with note pad and camera equipment, and she and Keasa set off on foot for the village.

"Have you always lived in the village?"

Keasa nodded. "Always. And we are raising our children in the peaceful Masai way."

"How many do you have?"

"Four. All boys. They are learning to be herdsmen."

They arrived half an hour later. The round grass huts were neatly placed to form the village. There was very little activity by anyone except the children because of the oppressive heat. Men who were almost naked hunkered in a group in the shade of a hut while women stood in open doorways and watched the approach of the tawny-haired American. Children came running from their games and circled Alex and Keasa, laughing and chattering in their native tongue, making walking difficult but fun.

They were curious little things, poking at her purse inquisitively and touching the soft cotton material of her shorts and blouse. She didn't mind. They were so lovely.

Finally the children hemmed them in so tightly that Alex laughingly stopped and sat on the dusty ground in their midst. Surprised, the children sat down as well, thinking this was a new game. Alex pulled things out of her purse and showed them to the children, explaining each item. Keasa translated Alex's explanations into Swahili. Her hairbrush fascinated them. She showed them how it slid through her silky hair and ended up with many curious dark fingers touching the soft strands in wonder. They might have seen that kind of hair before, but it was obviously the first time they'd touched it.

Grant approached the village on foot and stopped at its outskirts unnoticed as he watched the scene.

Alex's little pocket mirror was passed around, peered into, and exclaimed over. Her lipstick caused lots of giggles. Her camera was passed around and studied intently. She had a package of mints and gave one to each child. That was the biggest hit of the day.

The adults became curious as well and joined them. Most spoke no English, so Keasa made introductions in both languages. They were delightful, happy people, content with their lives, living the way the Masai had for countless centuries.

Then Alex saw Mary, smiling shyly and holding her baby in her arms. Alex got up and went to her. As she stared down at the tiny sleeping face, her heart melted. To think she had helped—even if just a little.

Mary didn't need a translator to tell her what Alex was saying as she took the baby into her arms and tenderly held her. The baby moved and burrowed against Alex's breast. For the first time, she realized how much she would love to have a baby.

The Australian's jaw grew taut as he watched the change in Alex's expression. It told him so much about her. And it pulled him up short. Alex mattered to him— mattered so much that he didn't want to see her hurt. But if she were to fall in love with a man who couldn't give her the children she wanted, she would certainly be hurt.

For the first time since his illness he was struck full force by the fact that he would never be able to father another child.

Carefully Alex returned the baby to Mary. Her eyes met the Masai girl's, and a quiet message of understanding passed between them, woman to woman.

Keasa showed her around the rest of the village, including the old hut the missionaries had used as a school. It was dilapidated now, and dirty on the inside from disuse. The children followed but, after a gentle command from Keasa in Swahili, didn't crowd them. Alex looked around the place thoughtfully. "Are these children getting any kind of education now at all?"

Keasa shook her head. "None. There is no one here qualified to teach."

"And your children?" She was curious because Jundi was educated and Keasa appeared to be also.

"They can all read and write," she said proudly, "both English and Swahili. Jundi and I taught them ourselves."

Alex wiped some black dirt from school tables still in the large hut and distastefully looked at her fingers. "Have you given any thought to teaching the other children?"

"But I am not qualified. . . ."

"Perhaps not, Keasa, but you're all they've got. If you could teach your own children to read and write, there's no reason you couldn't teach the others if you really wanted to."

Keasa sat on the edge of a table. "To be honest, I thought about reopening the school at one time, but we have no money for the necessary supplies. The children would need books and pencils and paper."

"What if someone provided the materials you need? Would you take on the job of teacher?" Alex asked suddenly, the germ of an idea beginning to form.

"But it would cost so much," Keasa protested.

Alex waved her hand. "Forget about that part of it. There's always a way to raise money if you're determined enough. Would you take on the job of teacher?" she asked again.

Keasa nodded slowly, then with more assurance. "Yes. Yes, I would. And I feel sure that Jundi would help when he could. He loves the children in the village and worries about their future. Times are changing, even for the Masai."

"Where would one be able to purchase the school supplies?"

"Seronera. It is not so far from Banagi by plane."

They left the hut just as Grant approached. He stopped, his enigmatic eyes on her. "I had a feeling you wouldn't have the patience to stay at Banagi all morning."

Alex's heart pumped harder at the sight of him. She was at a loss for something to say.

"I thought perhaps you wouldn't mind," Keasa told him.

"It's all right, Keasa. I knew she'd be safe with you." His attention returned to Alex. "Are you ready to go back?"

She got hold of herself. "I'm ready." She smiled at the African woman. "Thank you—

and I'll get back to you about what we discussed."

She and Grant walked side by side. He was friendly, but his emotional withdrawal was apparent. It hurt more this time than it had on the morning of the safari, because she was more involved than ever.

"How do you do that?" she asked suddenly.

He kept his eyes straight ahead. "Do what?"

"Make love to a woman at night and then act as though it had never happened the next day? You've got it down to an art."

He looked at the top of her shining head. "Perhaps it's because I regret having given in to a momentary impulse," he said softly. "Perhaps I'm afraid you'll begin to take things between us seriously and I don't want you to embarrass yourself." That was brutal, and he knew it.

Alex felt ill. She hadn't known what embarrassment was until this moment. "You needn't concern yourself. I told you that before. I'm a big girl."

His heart caught at the barely perceptible tremor in her voice. He had to resist the impulse to pull her into his arms. His fists clenched by his sides. "Good. Then we understand each other."

"Perfectly."

They walked on in silence. The only noises

were the soft thud of their footsteps on the dirt path and the buzz of insects. The air was hot and strangely heavy as it hung around them, unmoving.

When they reached the house, Alex stood on the first step and forced herself to look at the Australian. "I need to go to Seronera. How can I get there?"

He hesitated. "As it happens, I'm flying there later today. If you want to go with me, be ready by three o'clock."

She inclined her head stiffly and went into the house.

At precisely three o'clock she left her room dressed in a gathered white skirt and a delicate white blouse and met Grant in the living room. He had on tight buckskin-colored pants and a short-sleeved matching shirt with the top button undone and the knot of his tie casually loose.

Alex had done a lot of thinking since their morning talk. She was here to do a job. It had been unprofessional of her to get involved with Grant in the first place, but since she had, she intended to take his painful rejection like a lady. No scenes. No sulks. No tears. She would teach him the meaning of the word "civilized."

A smile curved her mouth but didn't reach her eyes. "Hello, Grant. I'm ready."

His brown eyes traveled appreciatively over her slender figure and tanned face and arms. He couldn't help it. She was so damned lovely. "Let's go, then."

Seronera was ninety minutes away by plane. It was like a small American city, with paved streets, sidewalks, and a variety of restaurants and shops. It had a small modern airport that handled light aircraft.

Grant and Alex touched down at Seronera's airport at four-thirty. He rented a jeep and dropped her off at a bookstore Keasa had recommended. He was obviously curious about why she had come to the city, but she didn't enlighten him. He took off to run his own errands.

The bookstore had everything she needed. School supplies covered entire racks. Alex found beginning readers and spellers, notebooks and pencils, crayons and drawing supplies. There were even novels she thought the children would enjoy having read to them in both English and Swahili.

She found books for Keasa on how to prepare lessons and handle classes. By the time she had finished, her bill was astronomical and her purchases filled a dozen large boxes. She made arrangements to have them trucked to Banagi, then waited in front of the store for Grant. He arrived almost immediately. She climbed into the rented jeep and he looked at her.

"Would you like to stay in town for dinner?" he asked.

Alex was feeling pleased about her successful buying binge, but her tone was cool when she replied: "That sounds nice."

They drove to a small French restaurant on the town's outskirts. It was dark and blissfully air-conditioned. When they were settled across from one another in a comfortable booth, her eyes wandered to the numerous other diners as they spoke in low voices.

"Surprised?" Grant asked.

She nodded. "I would never have expected to find a place like this here."

"Seronera is a tourist town mostly, but it's also the residence of a lot of foreigners who have business in Africa."

She put the crisp white linen napkin on her lap. "It's nice, but it's not Banagi," she said quietly.

He leaned back in his seat and studied her. "You really like it there, don't you?"

"More every day." Her eyes met his and the gap between them temporarily closed. "I can understand why you want so desperately to save it. I hope the magazine piece helps you."

A corner of his mouth lifted. "You know,

Alexandra, for two people who have come to know each other as . . . intimately . . . as we have, our conversations are sometimes very stilted."

Delicate color charmingly touched her cheeks. "I think the problem is that we don't really know each other at all, do we?"

"And yet we know each other so very well."

A waiter brought them some wine, then silently left. Alex stared at the rich, red liquid. She still hurt from the morning's rebuff but tried bravely to push that feeling aside so they could really talk. She liked talking to him. The fact was, she liked *him*. They had known each other such a short time, and yet there was a world of unspoken understanding between them. The Australian watched her expressive face curiously. "What are you thinking?"

Her eyes met his. "That I want to know everything about you, how you feel, what you believe, what kind of childhood you had, who your heroes are, your favorite books, your favorite poet. Everything."

He was lost in her clear gaze. "Sometimes you can know too much about a person, Alexandra."

"I disagree."

A smile touched his mouth. "Naturally."

She frowned. "I'm serious."

"So am I." He leaned forward and twined his fingers with hers. "There is a very strong attraction between us. We both know it. And it isn't just physical, though I'll admit," he conceded, "there isn't a part of me that doesn't want to make long, lingering love to every inch of you." He held her hand to his mouth and softly kissed the palm, his eyes on her melting ones.

She felt the same way. "Grant . . ."

"Ssshhh." His eyes were tender. "Do you realize that the first day we met, I thought that you might provide some nice physical entertainment for a few weeks, but within the day I realized I couldn't use you like that. No one was more surprised than I.

"I have a goal," he continued, "that becomes more blurry every time I'm with you, and that shouldn't be happening, but it is. I ask myself, what am I doing? Throwing away my hopes for my future, my self-respect, because I can't get a woman out of my mind?"

"What are you talking about?"

"Failure. And success. I've been convinced ever since Carolyn left me three years ago that she would eventually come back. I refuse to give my children the kind of insecure life I had. They deserve better than that. You, of all people, should realize how important a strong family life is for children. And I think she's getting ready, at last, to make a commitment to us. The signs are all there." His eyes held hers. "And now I'm not sure I want her back, and it's tearing me up inside. I desperately want what's best for my sons, but," he finished with quiet intensity, "I'm beginning to understand that what's best for them isn't necessarily what's best for me."

Alex slowly withdrew her hand from his and lowered her eyes. "I'm sorry," she said softly. "I understand some things now that I didn't before. You must think I'm an incredible fool. . . ."

A gentle finger tilted her chin so that she had no choice but to look into his eyes. "Haven't you heard what I've been saying to you, woman? I don't think you're a fool. You're one of the most delightful people I've ever known. Saying good-bye to you when the time comes is going to be one of the most difficult things I've ever done."

"Grant . . ." She swallowed and took a breath for courage. "If Carolyn doesn't come back, I'd like to stay here with you."

He didn't appear surprised by her words— rather, skeptical.

"For how long?"

"As long as you want me."

She hadn't thought any of this through. There was no logic. This was straight from the heart.

"Or until you get bored with life out here."

"I love Banagi," she protested. "That wouldn't happen."

He shook his head. "You weren't brought up for this kind of life. You'd never go the distance—whether you loved me or not."

"I really don't think that's for you to tell me."

"Alexandra," he said softly, "I've been here before. My ex-wife's background is a lot like yours. Like you, she had no doubts about handling life at Banagi because she was in love with me. She was wrong," he said bluntly. "And you're not even sure you're in love. What kind of chance does that give any future we might have?"

She shook her head helplessly. "I don't know. I don't know anything anymore, except that something in here," she touched her heart, "is telling me not to let you go without a fight."

He looked at her for a quiet moment. "But if you really *thought* about it," he finally said, "you'd run from me as fast as those long legs could carry you." He tried to lighten things up. "Besides, I fail your compatibility tests in one very important area."

She frowned at him. "What are you talking about?"

"I can't have any more children. Anyone with half an eye could see how much a family means to you."

She honestly hadn't thought about that. And it *did* mean a lot to her. She took a deep breath. "How much longer are the twins going to be visiting their mother?"

"A few more weeks. This is the first time they've seen her since the divorce."

"You mean you wouldn't let them . . . ?"

He shook his head. "No, nothing like that. Carolyn gave me the children because I wanted them. She didn't. She wasn't ready for motherhood, and it compounded all the other problems we were having. She was always ill at ease with the boys. But now she's apparently matured and wants a more active role in their lives."

Grant reached out and touched Alex's hand. "Truly, it's best if we stop things between us now, while we still can."

She nodded. "It's going to be difficult living together for the next three weeks."

"Not if we both realize the insanity of getting any more deeply involved."

"Sometimes insane situations are the most appealing," she suggested softly.

"And more often the most devastating."

He picked up his menu. "I think we should order."

The plane landed in darkness at Banagi, and they walked up the hill to the house, each lost in thought. The wall between them was securely in place once again.

The atmosphere was heavy with electricity and, for the first time since Alex had arrived, clouds blackened the sky and blocked the stars. Thunder sounded as a distant rumble that rolled through the sky, growing louder and louder until it was directly overhead.

The Australian stopped near the steps and stared into the darkness. "The rains are here," he finally said. "It's already raining over the plain about fifty miles away. It should be here in a few hours."

He looked down at the woman standing silently next to him. "I should warn you that thunderstorms here are probably more violent than any you've encountered before. The lightning seems closer, and the thunder is so loud at times that the earth vibrates with it."

She lifted her shoulders. "I'll probably sleep through it. It's been a long day." She turned and walked up the steps. "Good night." She spoke without looking at him and walked straight through the house to her room.

When the door had closed behind her she leaned against it and sighed. Had she said that the next three weeks were going to be difficult? That was an understatement.

He had tried to let her down twice that day. The first time by embarrassing her. The second by being nice. Once was sufficient. She was hurt and confused. She still had to face him tomorrow and the day after that and the day after that, until the article was done. Then she could leave Grant Adams and Banagi behind once and for all. One of these days she would look back on this short chapter in her life and wonder what all the fuss was about.

Wouldn't she?

Grant was right about the rains. As the storm neared Banagi it grew so loud that it made sleep impossible. The thunder cracked and roared. The earth shook. Lightning seemed to leap into the room with her. And when the rain finally fell, it poured in sheets, not drops, pounding the roof violently.

She tossed and turned fitfully. Her sheet was twisted into a knot before she finally gave up any attempt to rest. Opening her bedroom door a crack, she saw that the house was in darkness. Grant must have gone to bed. Quietly she left her room and went into the kitchen to rummage in the cupboards for chocolate. She found some and put it in a pan with milk to make cocoa. Then she wandered into the dark living room and leaned against the doorframe to watch nature at work. The night had grown surprisingly chilly and she rubbed her bare arms, wishing she had put on a warmer nightgown.

Remembering her cocoa, she went back to the kitchen and poured it into a mug.

A horrible crash of thunder unexpectedly split the sky. She jumped and the mug slipped from her fingers and shattered on the hard floor. She looked at it in dismay, then bent to pick up the large, jagged pieces.

Suddenly Grant was across from her, wordlessly helping. They each reached for the same piece and their hands touched. Alex lifted her eyes slowly to his, not wanting to look at him for fear of what he might see but unable to help herself.

They both straightened, the broken mug forgotten. He took her hand in his and looked down at it. Blood came from a small cut on the tip of a finger. It didn't hurt. She hadn't even known it was there. His dark eyes caught and held hers once more as he brought the finger to his mouth and gently sucked it.

Her breathing grew erratic at the blatant sensuality of the action. She wanted to strike him for doing this to her, and yet she didn't move. She couldn't take her eyes from the dark intensity of his. Without warning he released her hand, as though he suddenly realized what he was doing, and walked away from her across the kitchen. The trembling of her knees forced Alex into a chair.

Grant returned and kneeled before her, his sun-bleached head bent over her cut as he dabbed it and put on a small bandage. She reached out with her free hand to touch him but caught herself in time. Still without speaking, he put the things away, then brought two glasses of brandy to the table. "It will help you sleep," he explained tersely as he set one in front of her, then tossed his own back in one large swallow as he walked to the kitchen window and looked out at the raging elements.

Surprising herself, she polished hers off in two slightly smaller gulps and set the glass firmly back on the table.

"Go back to bed," he told her without turning around.

"But the mug . . ."

"I'll take care of it." His voice was tight. "Just get out of here. Now."

Alex rose so quickly at the urgency in his voice that her chair overturned. She righted it and walked from the kitchen with as much dignity as she could muster. But as soon as the door swung shut behind her, she ran through the house until she reached her room and was safe from herself and the Australian, behind her closed door.

She climbed into bed and hugged the pillow tightly to her. Was it too late for her to get out of Africa with her heart intact? The noise of the storm drowned her thoughts until the brandy did its numbing work and she was at last able to sleep.

Grant waited until he heard her door slam shut. His shoulders slumped slightly forward. Alex was a fever in his blood. An obsession. His fist crashed onto the counter before he spun around and strode from the house and into the storm, his face raised to the sky as the driving rain pelted his body.

Chapter Six

Two weeks passed. She and Grant treated
one another with cordial civility. Perhaps
that was best. Gathering information and
pictures for the magazine required most of
her time, energy, and attention. She loved
what she was doing and wanted to do the
best job she possibly could. For herself, of
course, but more for Grant. Funds for Banagi
had been low when she arrived. They had
dwindled even lower during the past few
weeks.

She had watched Grant work patiently
with the animals who came into the compound, nursing the ones he could back to
health, hurting over the ones he couldn't. He

was up until all hours making notes and going over them for his reports. He had some hopes of going on a lecture tour to bring in revenue.

The more she watched him, the more her common sense fell helplessly by the wayside. He was a good man whose strength arose from his sensitivity and, as she watched his gentle hands working with both people and animals, she grew to love him more and more. How could Carolyn have left a man like that?

This morning, as she walked down the veranda steps, she planned to spend the day with him at the animal compound. She stopped for a moment and breathed deeply of the fresh air, closing her eyes and turning her face toward the bright African sun. The heat was less intense since the rains had arrived.

Suddenly a small Thompson's gazelle ran up the hill past her, stopping several feet away to graze. Alex was surprised and delighted at its daring in coming so close to a human being, and she was careful to make no abrupt movements that would frighten the pretty baby away.

But as she watched the gazelle, an uneasiness crept over her. The hair on the back of her neck rose. And for good reason. Her narrowed, searching eyes spotted a lion crouched low in the grass not ten yards away. The gazelle had run to her for protection!

Alex swallowed in fear and remained still. The patient lion watched and waited, not knowing whether to ignore the unexpected obstacle of a human being and attack the gazelle anyway or simply to leave and find a more available source of nutrition.

It was a standoff. For nearly half an hour, as the gazelle munched unconcernedly behind her, glancing up only occasionally, Alex and the lion watched each other.

She didn't see the Australian start up the hill and stop, his face going pale at the danger she was in. Nor did she see him slowly retrace his steps and reappear, a rifle in his hands and aimed at the lion.

When the big cat finally rose, Alex's heart hammered against her chest and then stopped. This was the moment of truth. But it didn't spring into attack. It turned and nonchalantly trotted down the hill, bored with the game.

A shaken Alex sank to the ground, her hand over her pounding heart, and sat there, hardly daring to believe it was over.

Grant lowered the gun and exhaled.

The gazelle ate its way closer to Alex, whom it now perceived to be its friend, until it was only inches away. She held out an unsteady hand and let the little animal sniff before stroking its slickly smooth back.

It tensed at first, ready for flight, but soon realized that its new friend meant no harm and relaxed. Alex talked in a low, admittedly shaky, musical voice, stroking in a predictable pattern until the animal grew more used to it.

Grant walked up the hill and hunkered down next to her. "I see you've made a new conquest."

She smiled up at him. "There's no accounting for tastes, I suppose." She looked back at the gazelle. "Isn't he beautiful?"

He checked the animal over. "Yes, *she* is."

"Where do you suppose her mother is?"

"Dead, most likely."

She clicked her tongue in dismay. "Poor baby. What will happen now?"

"I'll keep her here and raise her until she's big enough to return to a herd."

Her eyes were sad as she looked up at him, her hand scratching the gazelle's ears. "And what kind of chance will she have for survival in the wild after being raised in captivity?"

It occurred to him to lie to her so she wouldn't worry, but he couldn't. "Fair. A herd might not even accept her."

Alex shook her head, her blue eyes darkened with emotion. "The Serengeti can be so cruel sometimes."

"It might seem cruel, I suppose. But in reality it's nature working at her best. Like nowhere else in the world."

A smile twisted his mouth as the gazelle dropped all hesitancy and licked Alex's sad face until she laughed. "Is there anything you don't feel motherly toward?" he asked.

Her smile faded as her eyes met his in a long look. "Yes," she said simply.

Their attention was reluctantly caught by the loud sound of an ancient truck straining its way to the Banagi hill from the direction of Seronera. Alex stood up and dusted off her jeans as she watched the vehicle approach. Grant walked partway and met it. He jumped onto the running board and spoke to the driver as the truck chugged the rest of the way up the hill, coming to a stop directly in front of Alex.

Grant stepped down and looked at her curiously. "Did you buy school supplies in Seronera?"

Her eyes lit up. "They're here!" She ran to the back of the truck and lifted the canvas flap. All the boxes were there. A little banged around, but all accounted for. "I was hoping they'd arrive before I left for the States."

Grant joined her. "For the village?"

"Keasa is going to teach the children to read and write."

He watched her in something close to wonder. He had been trying to talk Jundi's wife into doing that for years; within three weeks Alex had succeeded. "You're certainly leaving your mark on Banagi." He eyed the supplies. "This must have cost you a fortune."

"A small one, perhaps," she agreed, "but it's going to be worth every penny, don't you think?"

"And then some. The Masai children are naturally bright. They'll absorb knowledge like water."

She glanced around the side of the truck at the riverbed, now flowing shallowly with water. "Do you think the driver can get this thing across there and to the village?"

His eyes warmly touched the top of her head. "If he gets a running start. I'll talk to him."

The gazelle, apparently realizing that she was about to be thoughtlessly deserted, rubbed soulfully against Alex's leg. Alex, smiling apologetically, kneeled in front of her and scratched behind her ears. "What *am* I going to do with you?" she wondered aloud.

Grant overheard as he finished his conversation with the driver. "The first thing we should do is get her some milk before she gets dehydrated. There's no telling how long ago she had her last meal from her mother." He picked the unprotesting gazelle up under his arm and carried her into the house. Alex followed, pausing for just a moment as the truck plowed down the slight incline and across the riverbed. He made it.

She found Grant and the gazelle already in the kitchen. Kulu was preparing some powdered milk. When he finished, he poured it into a baby bottle. Grant took the bottle and sat on the floor with the gazelle.

The little thing was getting nervous at all this attention and clearly didn't have any idea what to do with the bottle of milk—in fact, found it threatening and backed away skittishly whenever Grant brought it near her mouth.

After a very patient fifteen minutes, his concern for the gazelle was obvious. He got to his feet and handed Alex the bottle. "You try. She has to eat something, and soon, or she'll die. Since she came to you for protection in the first place, perhaps she'll trust you."

Alex took up his position on the floor and set the bottle next to her leg, then sat quietly and waited for the gazelle to come to her, her eyes never leaving the lovely little thing.

The gazelle moved closer and closer until she rubbed against her human friend. Alex nuzzled her nose in the animal's neck and pulled the slight form onto her lap, stroking the smooth back and scratching the ears.

When she felt the time was right, she lifted the bottle and gently bumped the nipple against the gazelle's mouth, leaving behind a few drops of milk. The gazelle licked the moisture and the instinct for survival took over. With sharp movements of her head, she poked at the bottle until it slid into her mouth and she sucked on it.

Alex felt tears well in her eyes, and a smile curved her mouth. Grant hunkered down beside her and turned her face to his with an index finger under her chin. The look in his brown eyes warmed her. His mouth brushed hers. Then he was gone. She heard the screen door slam behind him. Kulu, at pains not to be caught staring, vigorously scoured the sink.

Curiouser and curiouser.

When Alex finally had the gazelle settled in the animal compound in a small, private pen, she headed for the village. The truck had been unloaded. Interested villagers stood outside the building where the boxes had been stacked, poking with fingers, prodding with toes. She commandeered several strong men to help her carry them inside, then invited everyone to watch as she unpacked the books, pencils, crayons, pads, and some learning toys she thought might be useful.

They were fascinated, the adults as much as the children. Keasa made her way through the crowd and kneeled beside Alex, her eyes alight as she saw what she had to work with. They were both like children themselves as they gleefully finished unpacking and shelving things.

Keasa clapped her hands and spoke in Swahili to the people, who nodded their understanding and left.

"What did you say?" Alex asked, rubbing her hands against her jeans.

"I told them that the school will be open tomorrow morning and that I expect to see all the children here, ready to learn, and any adults who would like to join in."

"Do you think many will show up?"

Keasa nodded. "All of the children, probably, and whatever adults can be spared from herding and gathering food." Keasa grew suddenly shy. "Will you be here tomorrow?"

Alex had thought about it. "No. You're the teacher, though I would love it if you'd let me know how everything goes."

"You may count on it."

Alex glanced at her watch. She had been there for hours. It was already time for dinner. "I have to get back to Banagi." She walked out of the hut into the bright sunlight. "Good luck!" she called over her shoulder, feeling unbelievably good about what she had helped bring to pass in the village.

She and Grant had dinner on the porch. Neither spoke much, but each was intensely aware of the other, as they always were. She felt his eyes on her throughout the meal but managed to keep hers downcast, afraid of what he might find there.

Afterward he worked at a small desk set in a corner of the living room, going over his notes and making new ones. Alex curled up on the couch with a paperback she had brought from the States, but she couldn't concentrate. Her eyes kept wandering to the back of Grant's head. What went on in that complex mind of his?

He turned unexpectedly, his eyes catching and holding hers. "It's been nearly four hours since your gazelle's last feeding. She should have one more bottle before morning."

Alex put her book down and went to the kitchen to get a bottle Kulu had already prepared. When she returned, Grant was standing by the door. "I'll go with you."

She hesitated, feeling vulnerable and not

wanting to expose herself. "That's not necessary. I don't mind going to the compound alone."

"I mind." He opened the door for her without further argument.

She lifted her shoulders and went out. He followed.

Grant had turned on the floodlights and they lit the compound. The animals stirred at the interruption and watched curiously as Alex entered the small pen holding the gazelle. "Hello, Chi," she said softly, smiling as the gazelle nuzzled the bottle and hungrily sucked. Alex sat on the ground cross-legged.

Grant stayed outside the pen and leaned his elbows on it as he watched. " 'Chi?' " he asked.

"It's Chinese for young or lucky. I think both apply in this case."

"Chi," he said again thoughtfully. "I like it."

The gazelle finished its meal in record time. Alex played with it a few minutes longer; then, brushing the dust from her clothes, she joined Grant. They stood together and watched as the gazelle, sleepy and satisfied, stretched out on its straw bed and relaxed.

"She's going to miss you."

"Do you really think so?"

He nodded. "You're her adopted mother."

After a moment's silence Alex asked, "And you? Will you miss me?"

His gaze touched the top of her shining head. "Yes."

Alex's eyes met his in a long, unwavering look. "Then don't let me go." She hadn't meant to say it, but there it was, and she didn't regret it. She didn't want to leave him. She couldn't imagine what her life would be like without him. A wasteland.

For the first time in weeks, unable to help himself, he pulled her into his arms and buried his face in her fragrant hair with a groan. "I have to," he said hoarsely.

She pulled away from him, knowing the reason. "Carolyn?"

His eyes lingered lovingly over every inch of her face. "No. She isn't even a factor in this anymore. I can't live with her now. Not with the way I feel about you."

Her heart leaped. Did that mean there was a chance? "Then why?"

"You really don't understand, do you?" He shook his head. "But why should you? I can't explain it to myself. It's crazy." He cupped her face in his hands and kissed her with a tenderness that brought tears to her eyes.

She put her hands over his and looked up

at him pleadingly. "Talk to me, Grant. I have a right to know what you're thinking. This is my life too."

He ran his hand through his hair distractedly and looked at the sky. Then his eyes came back to hers and stayed there. "I'm afraid of you," he said quietly. "Can you believe it? After all I've been through in my life, I'm afraid of a five-foot six-inch, 115-pound woman. Afraid of what you can do to me if I let myself love you the way I know I can and then lose you in the end."

"I love you too," she said almost in wonder, for the first time saying aloud what had been in her heart for a long time. "Why are you afraid?"

"Because of the power you hold in those soft hands to hurt me."

"But I wouldn't . . ."

He placed a silencing finger over her mouth. "If I were to ask you to marry me, right now, tonight, with your knowing it would mean you would never have a child of your own, what would your answer be?"

She wanted to be able to say she would give him an unqualified and jubilant *yes* . . . but she couldn't. She wanted children. And she was intelligent enough to realize that whether she loved him or not—and she most definitely, passionately, did—this was something she would have to think long and hard about.

He heard the answer in her silence and pulled her back into his arms. "That's why," he said quietly. "And thank you for not lying to me and saying it doesn't matter."

"Grant . . ."

He shook his head. "No more, Alexandra. We've said enough for tonight." His arms squeezed her lightly in a comforting gesture, then held her away from him. "Why don't you go on back to the house and go to bed?"

She swallowed, trying very hard not to cry. "What about you?"

He looked around the compound. "I have some things to do out here. I won't be long."

She didn't want to leave him, but it was obvious that he wanted to be alone, so she started up the hill, stopping halfway to look back at him as he stared unseeingly into the night. She had to drag herself the rest of the way up.

She lay in the dark for hours, her thoughts jumbled. Without thinking, only knowing what she felt, she finally rose and walked across the hall to Grant's room and tapped lightly on the door.

"Come."

She opened it and walked in, uncertain of

her welcome. Moonlight streaming through the uncurtained window shone on his bed. He was lying on his back, his hands behind his head, looking at her.

"What is it, Alexandra?"

It took a moment to find the courage to say the words. "I need to be near you tonight. I need you to hold me."

His dark eyes rested on her for a long moment. Then, "Come here."

She moved to his bed and sank down next to him on the mattress. They both lay on their sides. Grant pulled her back into his body spoon style. She curved into him with a perfect fit. He exhaled sharply at her movement and she felt his desire grow against her, but he made no attempt to make love to her—much as she wished he would. Instead he kissed the top of her ear and wrapped his arm around her stomach. "Goodnight."

"Goodnight, Grant," she whispered back, suddenly feeling very secure and warm and sleepy. Within minutes, like a child, she was sound asleep. Grant felt her even breathing. Slowly he closed his eyes as though in pain and pulled her even more tightly against him.

Chapter Seven

Dawn was just breaking when Alex awoke the next morning. Grant was standing shirtless in front of the window watching the sun rise, a ribbon at a time. She didn't move, but her eyes fastened on him. She would never tire of looking at him. He was the type of man who would grow more attractive with age rather than less.

The man sensed her eyes on him and turned. "How long have you been awake?"

"A few minutes. And you?"

"I never went to sleep."

Alex sat up and hugged her knees. "We need to talk some more."

He folded his arms across his chest and

135

leaned a shoulder against the window frame. "I think we've about said it all, Alexandra."

"But we love each other."

His expression was unchanged. "So it would appear."

She rocked herself slightly, not really sure where this dialogue was going. "Do you want more children?"

"Not for the sake of having more children." His dark eyes met and held hers. "But ask me if I want to see my child growing inside you—yes." His jaw grew taut. "It never mattered to me until now."

Alex chewed her lower lip, shocked at herself for what she was about to say. "We could live together, couldn't we? Without marriage? Just until we're really sure of our feelings."

Anger was in every line of his body, but his voice was cool. "I have no doubts about my feelings for you. And I will not live with you. You are offering me half when what I want is all or nothing. You're trying to leave yourself an opening from which to escape the relationship." He moved toward her and raised her chin so that she had to look him in the eye. "No, my love. And you are my love. I want you body and soul, completely and without reservations. When you can come to me like that, then we'll have something to talk about. But be aware, little one, that once you marry me, it's for life. There will be no divorce. I won't put myself through that again, nor my sons. Their stability will come either with you as their stepmother or with only me."

"Is that what this is all about?" she asked. "Your sons' security?"

He shook his head. "You know better than that, Alexandra. I've never loved a woman the way I love you. And before we cross the line that will make the two of us one, I have to know that I'm not going to wake up some morning and find you gone. I think I can handle almost anything but that."

Those were wonderful words to hear, but still she wavered. Grant was asking for total commitment. And she would be raising his sons by another woman. "So what happens from this moment on," she finally said, "is completely up to me."

"Completely. You have a lot to consider before you decide on marriage to me. What all this comes down to is not whether you love me. I think you do. But whether you love me enough to go the distance into an unpredictable future. You're the only one who can answer that, and it *must* be the right answer."

His mouth lightly brushed hers. "We have some reports of poachers. I'm going up in the plane to see if I can spot their camps. I'll be back before dinner."

"May I come?"

He paused, his back to her as he reached for the door. "Not this time. I'd like to be alone."

She heard the screen door slam shut. Alex closed her eyes and rubbed her aching temples. It should have been such a simple decision, but it wasn't. She had to reconsider what she had always thought her life would be like and what it would be like if she married the man she loved.

She spent most of the day sitting on the veranda writing. Hours flew by. Before she knew it dinner was ready and darkness was falling, and there was no sign of either Grant or his plane.

Kulu went home and Alex kept the food warming in the oven as long as she could. A small knot of worry grew inside her. Grant was always back when he said he would be. What if something had happened to him? What if the plane had crashed? He was all alone, and she didn't even know where to begin looking.

By midnight worry had turned to panic. The rains had returned. Thunder and lightning crashed overhead. Her eyes strained into the darkness. Grant was out there somewhere in the storm.

Not knowing what else to do, she went outside, crossed the wet and slippery rope bridge, climbed into the open jeep waiting on the riverbank, and headed for the Masai village. She noisily woke Jundi and Keasa. The sleepy couple let her into their home and sat her dripping-wet form down at a small table.

Her distressed eyes met and held Jundi's suddenly alert ones. "Grant isn't back," she told him. "We have to look for him."

He put a large calming hand on her shoulder. "First of all, he is probably fine. But regardless, there is nothing we can do tonight in this storm. We won't be able to look until tomorrow."

She leaped to her feet. "But we have to look tonight. He's probably hurt or he would have made it back on his own."

"But we don't know where to look, Miss. He could be anywhere on the plain."

Alex took a deep breath and got hold of herself. Getting upset wasn't going to help anything.

Sympathetic Keasa put her arms around Alex's slender shoulders. "He will be found and he will be just fine. You will see. He probably had engine trouble and decided to spend the night with his plane rather than try to make it back to Banagi on foot in the dark. You will spend the rest of the night with us, and tomorrow we will arrange for a search party."

"Thank you, Keasa," she said more calmly, rubbing her forehead. "But I have to get back to Banagi just in case he comes home." She turned to Jundi. "Will you organize the search tomorrow if he doesn't show up?"

"First thing."

She smiled wanly. There was nothing else to say.

When she got back to Banagi things were just as she had left them. No Grant. She sat on the couch in her-wet clothes and pushed the dripping hair out of her face. She sat rigidly straight, her hands clasped tightly in her lap. She felt so helpless. The man she loved was out there somewhere in trouble, and there was nothing she could do but wait until morning.

What she wouldn't give to have him there, beside her, right now. She could tell him what she had discovered. That she loved him and everything else paled into insignificance beside that one fact. That if she couldn't have *his* children, she didn't want any. That she wanted to marry him and help him with his work. Be his partner. That it didn't matter where or how they lived as long as they were together.

Why wasn't he there so she could tell him?

She was still sitting there, in the same position, at dawn the next morning when someone knocked on the screen door. The rains had stopped an hour earlier. She opened the door to find Kabloona standing there, his expression serious. "I understand the doctor is missing," he told her bluntly. "I wish to help find him."

She nodded. "Thank you. We're going to need all the help we can get. How did you hear?"

"I told you before, the Serengeti has a very efficient communications system. My family began searching several hours ago, when we first received word. If you wish to travel with me, you are welcome."

She looked over his shoulder at the rickety old jeep he used. "I'd appreciate it. I don't know where to tell you to begin looking, though. All I know is that he was told by someone—I don't know who—that there might be poachers somewhere. That's all I know, and it doesn't give us anything to go on. The plain is so huge."

"You are wrong. It gives us plenty to go on. I know where most of the new poachers' camps are. It is my business to know. If we fan out over the area we should be able to find him, even without help from the air."

As his eyes traveled over her bedraggled appearance, he felt an unaccustomed tug at his heartstrings. She had obviously been in the rain last night and allowed her skirt and blouse to dry on her. Her hair also had been allowed to dry without combing. Dark smudges under her eyes attested to a lack of sleep.

He reached out a comforting hand and gave her shoulder a squeeze. "I promise you we will find him, Miss." He didn't lie to her and say that everything would be fine. There was no telling what condition the doctor would be in, and she knew it as well as he did.

She patted his hand. "Thank you," she said quietly. "Before we go I should get his medical bag just in case we need it."

Kabloona waited for her in the jeep. Wordlessly they took off across the plain. Alex stared through binoculars until her eyes burned, but there was no sign of Grant or the plane.

As the hours passed and Kabloona toured all the poaching areas known to him, the knot of frustration and fear in her stomach grew until her body was tense with it.

It was late in the afternoon when Alex finally saw something. It looked like it might be the Cessna. "Over there!" she yelled with the binoculars pressed against her eyes, perched anxiously on the edge of her seat as the jeep bounced over the rutted plain. It was. Alex and Kabloona both leaped from the jeep and raced to the wreckage, not knowing what they would find.

Alex's heart stopped when she saw Grant pinned in the cockpit, unmoving.

Without a moment's hesitation, Kabloona took some rope out of the jeep and fastened one end to the door of the Cessna and the other end to the back of the jeep. Alex stood clear while he gunned the accelerator and ripped the door off the plane, then she climbed onto the wing to see if Grant was still alive.

He was, but the inside of the plane was like an oven from the constant beating of the sun on the unprotected and airless cockpit. She and the African managed to free Grant and drag him out onto the ground; he was still unconscious.

There was no reason to rejoice yet because there was no way to tell what the extent of his injuries was. One thing was obvious even to Alex, with her limited medical experience. One of his legs was broken. And there was a cut on his forehead. She looked up at Kabloona as they both bent over the Australian. "What now?" she asked.

"A splint." He strode off and returned moments later with two thick, flat sticks. While he held them in place, one on either side of the injured leg, Alex secured them with gauze she found in the medical bag. Then she cleaned his head wound and bandaged it.

Together they managed to lift Grant into the back of the jeep with as little movement as possible. Then they started the long drive to the hospital at Seronera. Alex sat in back with Grant, his head in her lap, stroking his hair and staring down at his feverish face. Occasionally she would soak a cloth in cool water from Kabloona's jug and hold it on Grant's forehead. Her emotions were still under tight control. If only he would open his eyes and look at her. . . .

Kabloona pushed the jeep to the maximum. They pulled up to the emergency entrance at the hospital, then had to stand back while strangers in white coats lifted Grant onto a stretcher and took him away. Alex followed as far as they would allow her but got turned back at the emergency examining room.

A nurse at the admitting desk asked the necessary questions and then all that was left to do was wait. She found Kabloona in a sitting room.

"Word has gone out to Banagi that he has been found," he told her.

She sat down next to him. "Thank you. Thank you for everything."

The large African inclined his head. "The doctor and I do not share all the same views, but I respect him, as I believe he respects me."

She nodded but was unable to think clearly. Leaning forward, her elbows on her knees, she rested her face against her palms and rubbed her forehead with trembling fingers.

The African saw the hospital doctor approach before she did and touched her shoulder. They rose together. Alex searched the man's face for some sign of what the news would be but found nothing there. Her throat closed with anxiety.

"You are the two who brought Dr. Adams in?" he asked.

Alex nodded. "How is he?"

"Dehydrated, concussed, suffering from a broken leg, broken ribs, and heat exhaustion, but he'll recover."

She put her hand over her mouth, and at last the tears spilled hotly onto her cheeks. He would be all right.

Kabloona put his arm around her shoulders. "Thank you, Doctor."

The man smiled, happy to be able to deliver good news. "And if your name is Alexandra, young lady, he would like to see you. He's been moved to room 412."

She quickly swiped at her damp cheeks with the back of her hand and brushed down her badly wrinkled clothes as best she could, then looked anxiously at the African. "Do I look all right, Kabloona?"

He smiled down at her. "You are a mess, but I don't expect the doctor will think so."

Beaming, she kissed him on the cheek. "Thank you—for everything."

He bowed slightly. "You are most welcome. I hope to see you again." He turned to leave, but then he hesitated. "And give my regards to your man."

Alex took the elevator to the fourth floor and found Grant's room. She stood outside it for a moment and took a deep, calming breath, then opened the door slowly and peered in.

Grant was in bed, his eyes closed. His leg was in a cast up to his thigh. His ribs were cleanly bandaged. The cut on his forehead had a patch bandage.

With her heart in her eyes, she moved to the side of the bed and stared down at him. She had come so close to losing him forever. To think it had taken a near tragedy like this to make her realize how much he meant to her.

Grant felt her presence and opened his eyes. A tremulous smile curved her mouth. "Hello," she said softly.

His eyes traveled over her and a corner of his own mouth lifted. "You're a mess."

"So I've been told. And it's all your fault. What happened?"

"A bird flew into the plane. The engine stalled and I had to crash-land. I don't remember much after that." He took her hand in his and gave a gentle tug. "Kiss me, woman."

She leaned over and touched her mouth softly to his, afraid of hurting him further. His hand tangled in her hair and pressed her lips more firmly to his.

A hot tear fell on his cheek. He looked at Alex in gentle surprise and wiped her stained cheeks with his thumbs as he held her face in his hands. "What's this? I didn't think you ever cried."

She buried her face in his neck, and his arms automatically went around her slender, shaking shoulders, holding her as close to him as his injuries would allow. "Alexandra?"

She struggled to get hold of herself. "I was so afraid I'd lost you," she mumbled into his neck. "I think I could survive anything but that."

He kissed her hair and closed his eyes. A smile curved his handsome mouth. "Then you love me enough."

The arms around her slackened. With a final hiccough, Alex straightened and looked down into Grant's sleeping face. The drugs were taking effect.

His words stayed with her. She did love him enough. There was no question in her mind. She pulled up a chair and sat by his bed, holding his hand until a nurse came in and asked her to leave.

She wanted to stay in Seronera with him, but she knew there were things at Banagi that needed to be done. Exhausted, she took a taxi to the airport and arranged to have herself flown back.

Little did she know what awaited her.

Chapter Eight

Alex wearily made her way up the Banagi hill with the moon as her light. It was full and bright, but after thirty-six hours with no sleep and lots of anxiety, she was incapable of enjoying it. All she wanted to do was bathe and fall into bed. Now that she knew Grant would be all right, she could sleep.

Lights were on inside the house. That didn't surprise her. She assumed Jundi was waiting for her, or perhaps the cook had been in a hurry and had forgotten to turn them off. She made it up the steps and through the screen door.

A woman sitting on the couch playing

solitaire looked up expectantly—a lovely, elegant woman with fashionably short hair framing an intelligent, interesting face. Alex knew without asking who she was.

Her heart sank. Carolyn was back.

The other woman rose gracefully to her feet, her expectant look fading and a curious one replacing it. "I'm Carolyn Adams. And you're . . . ?"

"Alexandra Hollister."

Carolyn extended her hand in a friendly fashion, not showing by so much as the bat of an eyelash that the name meant anything to her. She looked Alex over thoroughly. "You appear to have had a rough day."

"A couple of them."

Carolyn looked past Alex's shoulder. "Is Grant with you?"

"He's going to be in the hospital for a few more days." When Carolyn paled, Alex realized immediately that the woman hadn't known a thing. She hadn't come because she'd heard that Grant was missing.

Alex went to her side and helped her onto the couch. "I'm sorry, Carolyn. I assumed that's why you were here—that Jundi or someone had gotten word to you about his accident. He was in a plane crash, but his injuries aren't serious. He'll be completely back to normal in a few months."

"I should be with him . . ."

The knife went in a little. "He's on medication. Even if you went there tonight, he wouldn't know. I think you should wait for a day or two."

Carolyn's smoky grey eyes met Alex's dark blue ones. "You wouldn't just say that to keep me away from him, would you?"

She held the woman's gaze unwaveringly. "No."

Carolyn believed her and relaxed. Her attention returned to Alex's bedraggled appearance. "I'm sure you're aching to get cleaned up. Why don't you do that, and I'll fix you some tea."

Oh, but they were being civilized. Alex's intuition told her that Carolyn knew perfectly well she was the new woman in her ex-husband's life. Alex's intuition also told her that Carolyn didn't like it at all, and that the tea was really an invitation to talk.

She got wearily to her feet. "Thank you. I won't be too long."

A few minutes later she lowered herself into a luxurious, steaming bubble bath and didn't emerge until half an hour later, flushed and sleepier than ever. She put on a modest, puffed-sleeve nightgown. She wasn't about to get dressed, even for a confrontation with Carolyn.

Carolyn was waiting for her in the living

room. She smiled as Alex took a chair across from her and poured herself a cup of tea. "I made it strong. Hope you don't mind. Grant always loved my tea."

The knife went in a little further. Alex sipped, then set the cup back in the saucer. "It's perfect."

The two women sat in uncomfortable silence. Carolyn finally broke it. "Keasa wrote me about you," she said abruptly.

Alex forced herself to look at the woman. "What did she say?"

"That Grant was falling in love with you."

Alex closed her eyes and let out a long breath. She never would have believed it of Keasa.

"Oh, don't go feeling betrayed. She's been writing to me ever since I left to keep me up-to-date on my boys' progress and what was happening here. She was happy for Grant because she thinks you're a nice person, and she assumed I would be as well." She paused. "Has he asked you to marry him?"

Alex didn't dissemble. "Yes."

"And did you accept?"

"Not yet. Not officially. But I intend to."

"Then I'm in time!" Carolyn breathed, more to herself than to Alex.

"In time for what?"

"To stop this craziness!" She got to her feet

and paced around the room, stopping at last before Alex. "We've been apart for three years. That's longer than we were married. I think I've known all along that I still loved him, but I didn't realize how much until I got that letter. That's when it hit me that if he went through with another marriage I would have lost him completely."

"Not completely," Alex disagreed. "Never completely, because of the twins."

Carolyn looked down at her. Alex had on no make-up, and yet her honey-tanned skin was clear and smooth. Her dark lashes and brows contrasted strikingly with her tawny hair. Carolyn hadn't expected her to be so lovely. Or so likable. "Miss Hollister, you don't understand. I want things to be the way they were. I want my husband back, and I expect you to do the honorable thing and clear out of his life."

Alex unconsciously straightened her shoulders. "Grant is your *ex*-husband."

Carolyn was unfazed. "He never wanted the divorce, you know. I was the one who pushed for it. He still loved me."

"But he doesn't love you anymore," Alex told her quietly. She wasn't being malicious. Only truthful.

Carolyn returned to the couch and sat down heavily. "I know that." She looked at Alex. "But if you were to leave and give me a chance to work things out with him, I believe he *could* love me àgain. I'm the mother of his children."

The knife was now in up to the hilt. That was certainly something she could never take away from her. "Why should I do that? Why would I *want* to?"

Carolyn chewed her lower lip. This was obviously difficult for her. "If Grant doesn't let me back into his life, I'll take his sons away from him so fast it will make his head spin. And I think you've been around him long enough to understand how much he loves those boys and how much they mean to him."

Alex studied her fingernails. "And if he marries me?"

"He won't even get visitation rights. He hasn't the money or the time to fight me." She looked pleadingly at Alex. "Please, don't make me do that. Besides, do you honestly believe he could be happy with you if he knew you cost him his sons?"

Alex narrowed her eyes at the woman. "I think you are a person of the lowest sort to use children that way. It's vicious. From what I've heard, they love him as much as he loves them. Your children would end up suffering as well."

Carolyn seemed to find it necessary to defend herself. "I'm not as bad as you think, really. I'm just using whatever ammunition I have to fight for what I want. Whether or not the children—and Grant for that matter —suffer is entirely up to you."

Alex ran her hand tiredly through her damp hair. "I can't give him up." Her voice cracked on the words. "I love him."

Carolyn leaned forward and touched her hand. "It's *because* you love him that you will."

Alex rose slowly to her feet. "Look. I've had a very rough day and a half. I'm too tired right now to deal with this rationally. I just can't."

Carolyn nodded. "I understand. I probably should have waited until tomorrow, but I felt I had to be honest with you."

Alex nodded and went to her room. Without turning on the light, she slid between the sheets, sure she'd never get to sleep. But she was wrong. Exhaustion dulled her ability to think, and within minutes she sank into a deep and dreamless sleep.

When she opened her eyes the next morning, she lay on her back for a long time, staring at the ceiling as the conversation with Carolyn played over and over again in her mind. Her fists clenched and unclenched by her sides in anguish.

She owed Carolyn nothing. The woman

had walked out on Grant. Not the other way around. But the boys. She could hear them outside playing noisily. They must have been sleeping last night. How could she live with herself? She knew what she should do. The only question was whether she was strong enough to give up this wonderful man and the beauty they had found together.

She heard a plane overhead. A glance at the bedside clock told her it was the one she had hired to take her back to Seronera. Back to Grant.

With leaded movements she brushed out her tawny hair and dressed in a gathered aqua skirt and white blouse.

Carolyn was standing in front of the screen door in the living room waiting for her. She turned nervously at Alex's approach.

"Did you think about our conversation last night?" she asked.

A corner of Alex's lovely mouth lifted in ironic amusement. "How could I think about anything else?"

"And?" Carolyn pressed.

"And," she exhaled wearily, "I know what I *should* do. I just don't know if I can."

The twins chose that moment to race into the living room from the veranda, covered with dust and full of laughter. The laughter faded when they saw Alex, and their brown eyes grew serious. Brown eyes exactly like their father's. Alex swallowed. They were beautiful children.

Both of them wiped dirty hands on still dirtier shorts and walked up to her, arms extended. She shook their hands, a tremulous smile touching her lips. "Which one is Timmy?"

The one on the right beamed at hearing his name. "I am, and the older."

"By ten minutes," the other hastened to add. "He always says that like it's some big deal," Craig explained in appropriately disgusted five-year-old fashion.

"Is our daddy really okay?" Timmy asked. "Carolyn said he was in an accident." It was a bit of a shock to hear their mother called by her first name.

Alex hunkered down in front of them, touched by the worry on their streaked faces. "He's just fine. And he'll probably be home in a week or so. You'll be able to see for yourselves."

"All right!" they shouted in unison and, all else forgotten, raced back outside.

Alex straightened. Her smile faded. "I'm going to see Grant now. You're welcome to fly there with me."

"No," Carolyn said quietly, actually feeling some of the pain of the other woman. "I think I'll wait. The two of you have a lot to discuss. You don't need me peering over your shoulder."

Alex inclined her head and walked past her, down the veranda steps, and out to the waiting plane. She was silent for the entire flight. The pilot glanced across at her occasionally, not only because she was pleasant to look at but because something was obviously very wrong.

She couldn't think of anything but Grant and how she was going to tell him she was leaving on schedule the next day for the United States.

When she finally arrived at the hospital, she stood outside his door to collect herself. She forced a smile, straightened her shoulders, took a deep breath, and walked in.

He turned his head on the pillow, and the love that filled his eyes at the sight of her was nearly her undoing. Wordlessly she moved to the side of his bed and kissed him full on the mouth. All the yearning and pain were there for him to feel.

When she lifted her head, his eyes narrowed on her. "What's all that about?"

Her lips parted, but no words came out. She straightened and walked to the hospital room window to stare out. A careless hand pushed the tawny hair away from her face. "How are you feeling today?"

"Like I was in a plane crash." He watched the back of her head, a very bad feeling forming in the pit of his stomach. "Alexandra, what's wrong? I know you too well."

Still she didn't look at him. On the way to the hospital she had thought of a hundred different ways to tell him good-bye, but now that she was actually here, she couldn't remember one of them.

"I've decided not to stay in Africa," she ended up blurting out. "You were right when you said there were too many problems."

"Look at me, Alexandra."

She turned slowly until her eyes met his.

"If you want out of my life," he said quietly, "you're going to have to be more specific about the reasons."

She dropped her gaze.

"Look at me," he ordered again.

Her eyes flashed at him. "All right!"

"Now, explain."

"I just want to go home. I want to have a normal life with a normal man who works nine to five, if I ever decide to marry. And . . . and I want my own family."

His expression gave nothing away as he held her gaze. "You're lying," he finally said. "Those are all very good reasons. Very legitimate. But they're not yours. What's the real story?"

Her lower lip trembled annoyingly. She

caught it between her teeth. For years she hadn't shed a tear, but during the last few days she seemed to be making up for it. Sitting on the edge of the hospital bed, she leaned over and rested her cheek on his shoulder. "Just hold me, Grant."

His arms closed comfortingly around her. They sat like that for a long time. Alex took a deep breath. "When I left you last night, I went home to Banagi. Carolyn was there, with your sons. She wants you to take her back."

Grant's arms involuntarily tightened at the mention of his ex-wife's name. "She what?"

Alex straightened. "She wants to live with you again."

His jaw grew taut. For three years he had hoped Carolyn would change her mind and come back so that they could be a family again. It hadn't mattered that he wasn't in love with her anymore, because he wasn't in love with anyone. But now there was Alex. The news was bittersweet.

"I met Craig and Timmy this morning," she added. "They're just like you."

His face softened at the mention of their names, but then he remembered his ex-wife again. "What did Carolyn say to you?"

Alex shrugged. "Lots of things. But the gist of it all is that she realizes she was wrong to leave you. She's still in love with you and hopes to be able to win you back."

"And if I marry you?"

Alex smiled, but there was no amusement in it. "I asked that very question. If you marry me, she'll take the boys and make sure that you don't even have visitation rights."

"I'll take her to court."

Alex rose and walked back to the window. "You don't want to put your children through that. I don't want you to. And you'd never win. Everything is in her favor."

The Australian watched the play of light on her shining hair. "I can't just let you go," he said hoarsely.

"You have to. Just as I have to let you go. If we blindly follow our hearts, eventually we'll end up hating each other. You, because you won't have your children. Me, because of guilt. Your only option is to reconcile with Carolyn and try to get back what the two of you once had." She shook her head. "You know, I'd like to hate her for this, but I can't. If I were in her place I'd do exactly the same thing."

Grant leaned back on his pillows and stared unseeingly at the ceiling. He knew she was right, but that didn't make it any easier. He loved her more than he'd ever thought himself capable of loving another human being. She was as much a part of him as breathing. And he couldn't have her.

Alex walked to the door. Her hand was on the knob, but she couldn't resist looking at him one last time. Their eyes met and held, saying more in a few seconds than they could have in a lifetime of words.

Then she left. Her light perfume lingered in the air, filling Grant's senses. He closed his eyes tightly. A single tear rolled from the corner of his eye.

Chapter Nine

Time passed. The magazine came out with Alex's article and pages of magnificent color photographs. It was well received, and she had heard that contributions to Banagi were pouring in.

Alex was working hard to get her life back in order. But sometimes late at night, when all was quiet, she thought of Grant with Carolyn and her heart would slowly break all over again.

She had confided in no one, and so it was with complete innocence that her mother visited her one day with the news that Grant would be lecturing students of zoology and veterinary medicine at Northwestern University. It was less than an hour's drive from her home. She knew she shouldn't go. But the need to see him overwhelmed every other consideration.

At eight o'clock that evening, despite heavy snow, she was in the lecture hall with hundreds of students and interested spectators, her eyes glued to the podium, waiting. Seconds dragged by.

And then he was there. Her heart caught at the sight of him, his dark skin contrasting with his sun-bleached hair and crisp white shirt, the brown eyes looking out over his audience as they applauded him. He wore his tan suede jacket and tie as easily as he wore his jeans in Africa. His voice was clear and strong, with its attractive accent. He wasn't at all nervous as he joked with the crowd and conversed rather than lectured. He was as natural as if he were speaking to friends.

Alex tried to concentrate on what he was saying, but she couldn't. She just looked, trying hard to memorize every little detail for future recall.

He was well into his talk when he saw her. He stopped in the middle of a sentence and stared for a full fifteen seconds before he recovered himself and continued. But his eyes stayed on her. Afraid that if he looked away she'd disappear.

As soon as he finished, people poured onto the dais to meet him and ask questions, but he pushed his way through them to get to Alex. Just as she reached the door he caught her and grabbed her arm. "Don't go," he said urgently.

She knew she should but nodded helplessly. Holding her arm, he led her back through the hall to the dais, where he spent the next half hour answering questions and shaking hands. At the first opportunity, he gathered his papers and briefcase, helped her into her coat, and walked her outside where at last they were alone.

They stopped under a streetlamp. Grant put an index finger under her chin and drank in the sight of her. "You look wonderful," he finally said.

A smile touched her mouth. "So do you." She raised a hand and touched the dark circles under his eyes. "A little tired, perhaps, but wonderful."

He put his hand over hers and held it against his face. "Have dinner with me."

She pulled her hand back but her eyes remained locked with his. "I really don't think we should."

"I'm not asking you to make love," he said quietly. "I'm only asking you to be with me for a few hours while I'm here."

"All right," she finally agreed. "Dinner."

He found a small French restaurant. They were ushered to a quiet, dimly lit table in the back where they could talk undisturbed. Grant ordered a bottle of wine. When it came, he raised his glass to her in a silent salute.

He leaned back in his chair and looked at her across the table. "It would appear that I owe you an apology for some sarcastic remarks I made on the day we met. The magazine piece you did on Banagi was truthful, hardhitting, and vivid. We've gotten lots of backing because of it."

"Thank you. I was pleased with it myself. I'm hoping to do a little more writing in that area, now that I know I can handle it."

A corner of his mouth lifted. "I think we're having one of our stilted conversations again."

She nodded her tawny head. "You're right. But there's no way around it this time."

"There is if we say what we feel and ask what we want to ask."

He was right. She leaped in with both feet. "How's Carolyn?"

He raised his glass to her with a half-smile. "Now that's breaking the ice." He took a sip and exhaled. "She's fine. We're trying hard to work things out between us for the boys' sakes, but it hasn't been easy."

"Have you remarried yet?"

"No," he said quietly. "And you? Is there anyone special in your life?"

She shrugged. "I see different men from time to time, but there's no one special."

He leaned forward and held her hand in his, rubbing its smoothness with his thumb. "I think about you all the time."

She closed her eyes and swallowed. "I think about you too."

"I thought it would get easier as time went on, but it isn't working out that way."

"For me either."

Grant wanted to pull her into his arms and kiss that stricken look from her lovely face, but that would only lead them both into disaster. No matter how much he wanted Alexandra—no matter how much he loved her—he had given his word to Carolyn that he would try to work things out with her. He intended to keep it. If Alex hadn't shown up at the university that night, he wouldn't have sought her out though he was well aware that she lived nearby. Not seeing her at all seemed somehow less painful.

Alex suddenly stood up. "Grant, this was a mistake. You stay here. I'll take a taxi to my car." Without another word she rushed out of the restaurant. Grant threw some money onto the table and strode after her. He found her standing in the snow just outside. It was beginning to come down again, heavily. She

frantically signaled a taxi that cruised by
but to no avail.

Grant stepped in front of her and buttoned
up her flapping coat with infinite gentleness.
Wordlessly he took her arm and led her to his
car. She spoke only to point out where she
was parked. When they finally found her car,
she thanked him politely and got out, but he
couldn't leave it at that. He got out also and
opened the door of her sports car for her.

As she stood before him, he raised her face
to his and stared into the depths of her dark
eyes. Strong winds blew the stinging snow
into their faces, but neither noticed. A long
strand of hair blew across Alex's mouth.
Grant brushed it away with a gentle finger,
then slowly outlined her mouth with his
thumb as his hands cupped her face. Their
lips were inches apart, being drawn irresisti-
bly nearer. She could feel his warm breath
on her cold face.

Suddenly Grant got hold of himself. "No,"
he whispered harshly. "No!"

Alex took a shaky deep breath and held
onto the car door to support her suddenly
weak legs.

"Get in the car."

She obeyed. He closed the door firmly, then
stood in the snow while she started the cold
engine and turned on the windshield wipers
to knock the snow off. Without a backward

glance, she put the little car in gear and started the drive home. The anguish she had felt when she first realized that she and Grant weren't meant to be together consumed her anew. Her chest ached with it. Was this what she had to look forward to for the rest of her life? Would the pain of her first love ever go away?

The Australian stood in the snow and watched until the red glow of Alex's taillights disappeared. He knew the answer to the question Alex had just asked herself.

There was nothing ordinary about what they felt for one another. It wasn't something that was going to go away with a wave of a magic wand or wishful thinking. They were in each other's blood. No one could ever take that away from them. They were meant to be together. He knew it with a certainty that wouldn't be denied. Maybe not this year, or the next, or the next. But eventually they would be together.

He had to believe that. It kept him going.

Chapter Ten

Weeks went by. Alex got on with things as best she could. It was late one evening when there was a knock at her door. She was in a robe in front of her fireplace reading a book. Assuming it was one of her parents stopping by for a late-night cup of cocoa, she opened it smiling. But the smile faded when she found Carolyn on her doorstep, a child on either side, each holding a small suitcase.

Carolyn walked in without being invited and immediately went to the fireplace to warm her hands. Timmy and Craig just stood there looking sleepy and disoriented. "Close the door, would you?" she asked. "You're letting all the cold air in."

Alex automatically did as she was told. "What are you doing here?"

Carolyn glanced meaningfully at the boys. "We'll talk later. Right now, have you got a place for the twins to lie down? They've been traveling since yesterday."

Timmy smiled wanly up at her, his little face pale and tired. Alex kneeled in front of him and undid his coat and hat and helped him off with his mittens. Craig moved in front of her and patiently waited for her to take care of him as well. "Would you like some cocoa, or something to eat?" she asked. Both shook their heads no.

Without any assistance from their mother, Alex led them to an extra bedroom and helped them get into their pajamas. Then she tucked them into the cozily quilted double bed. Timmy wrapped his arms around her neck and gave her a hug. Craig was more cautious but allowed her to kiss his warm cheek. "Have you ever been a mommy before?"

What an odd question. "No. No, I haven't had that pleasure."

Craig's eyes narrowed on her, just the way his father's had so many times. "Do you want to be?"

"Yes." She tilted her head to one side. "Why do you ask?"

He rolled onto his side away from her. "No reason."

Timmy gave her a secret smile, but he had nothing to say. His eyelids drifted down and soon they were both sound asleep.

By the time Alex returned to the living room, Carolyn had made herself at home. Her coat lay across the couch and she cradled a cup of hot coffee in her hands as she sat curled up on the rug in front of the fireplace.

Alex pulled her robe around herself and sat down on the couch. "All right, Carolyn, they're asleep. Now, what's going on?"

The other woman eyed her. "It's very simple, really. You win."

"Win what?"

"Everything. Grant and the twins."

Alex looked at her out of suspicious blue eyes. "I don't understand."

"Then let me spell it out for you. Grant doesn't want me. He can't even touch me without flinching as though it's some distasteful task. He can't make love to me." She shook her head. "Oh, he tried. It was part of our agreement to try to get things back the way they were. But he couldn't." She looked up at Alex out of sad eyes. "Because I wasn't you."

"He said that?"

"Of course not. But contrary to what you

might believe, I'm neither stupid nor insensitive. My one hope going into this was that I could win him back. But I can't. Perhaps if he had loved me in the beginning the way he loves you I would never have left him."

Alex couldn't believe what she was hearing. She didn't know whether to laugh or cry. "You mean you're going to let us be together, and you're not going to fight him over custody of the boys?"

"I'm giving them to you—from Africa, with love. Think of them as my wedding gift."

Alex leaned forward, as though by getting that much closer she could understand this woman better. "Carolyn, these are your children we're talking about. Not toasters."

She looked Alex right in the eye. "I know exactly what we're talking about. And I know exactly what you're thinking. But listen to what I have to say before you judge me." She stared into the fire. "I never wanted children. Grant was the one anxious to have a family. Perhaps somewhere deep inside he knew . . ." She shrugged her shoulders dismissingly. "That's neither here nor there. I love Craig and Timmy. They're my babies. But there are some women in this world, believe it or not, who have no business mothering anybody. It's all I can do to look after myself, much less two five-year-olds. I have no patience with them. I make them miserable, and they make me miserable. But I'm good with them on short visits. And short visits are all I'm going to ask of you."

Alex watched her profile, not quite trusting what she was hearing. "Carolyn, isn't it possible that this is a heat-of-the-moment decision? You could turn around and change your mind tomorrow. Once you get away from the children and start missing them . . ."

The other woman held up her hand. "You're not listening to me. Believe me when I say that one of the happiest times of my life was right after I left Grant and the twins in Africa and headed for Australia and the life I had there before I got married. I missed Grant. And I admit I missed the twins a little. But mostly I was relieved not to have that responsibility anymore."

"But you were going to fight for custody of them."

"Because I wanted Grant. Not the twins. I was using them to get to him. I told you that and I make no apologies for it. It just didn't work out, that's all." She shook her head, smiling at some private joke. "I don't know. Perhaps I'm glad deep down that it didn't. I really don't like Banagi. The dirt, the heat, the animals. But I thought if that was the only place I could have him, I'd give it one more try." She shrugged. "That's life, I suppose."

Alex leaned back on the couch, picking up a needlepoint pillow and hugging it to her, afraid to believe this was really happening. "So what now?"

"So now I leave the boys in your care. All Grant knows is that I've left Africa with them. I really didn't need to bring them all the way here, but I wanted to, as sort of a symbolic gesture for myself. I wanted to be the one to give you my children. And when you return to Africa with the twins, he'll understand immediately what has happened and hopefully have a kind thought for me."

Carolyn looked at her watch and rose. She was silent as she put her coat on.

Alex rose also, tossing the pillow back onto the couch and sinking her hands deep into the pockets of her robe. "Where are you going?"

"I have a flight out of O'Hare in ninety minutes. I don't want to miss it."

Alex walked Carolyn to the door and opened it for her, then pulled the robe more securely around herself against the cold as she watched the woman walk down the driveway to her rented car. "Carolyn!" she called suddenly.

Carolyn stopped and turned.

"Thank you. I'll take good care of your children. They'll be as my own."

"I know that," Carolyn called back. "You don't think I'd leave them with just anybody, do you?" With a final careless wave, she was gone.

Alex shut the door thoughtfully. It was hard to comprehend that suddenly everything in her life was right.

She stole quietly into the bedroom and stood in the darkness watching the twins sleep. She pushed first Timmy's and then Craig's hair out of their faces. "I'll be a good mommy," she promised them softly. "We're going to be the happiest family that ever was. You'll see. You just inherited two wonderful grandparents and four crazy uncles who are going to love you as much as your daddy and I do."

Craig opened sleep-filled eyes. "Is Carolyn gone?" he asked.

"Yes."

"Can we go back to Daddy now?"

"Yes."

He nodded and yawned as he buried his nose back in the pillow. "Good. I miss him."

She kissed the side of his head. "Me too, Craig. Me too."

A few days later the plane she rented in Arusha dipped low over Banagi, scattering the animals before landing on the plain and taxiing to a halt near the Banagi hill.

Grant must have heard the plane and thought it was Carolyn returning with the boys, because he came racing down the hill toward them. The twins saw him and, with Alex's permission, leaped from the plane and ran into his waiting arms.

She thanked the pilot and stepped out herself. Grant looked over the boys' heads and caught his first glimpse of her. His carved face was expressionless as he straightened. "Alexandra." They just stood there, eyes locked.

The twins looked at each other and shrugged at the strange behavior of adults, then raced up the hill.

Grant took a step toward her, and that was all Alex needed. She ran to him and threw herself into his open arms. He held her tightly to his heart and closed his eyes.

Hardly able to believe she was really there, he held her away from him and looked his fill. Alex did the same thing. Finally he crushed her to him again. "Oh, God," he groaned as he buried his face in her hair and inhaled deeply of the fragrance he had grown to love. "I never thought this day would come." He looked down at her. "How did you get the boys? Did Carolyn go to you when she left here?"

She nodded. "It was very difficult for her," she said quietly. "I don't know that I would have had that much courage had the situations been reversed."

"I'll always be grateful to her." With their arms around one another they walked up the hill. Keasa stood near the house with Jundi, beaming. She and Alex hugged. Then Keasa turned to Grant. "I have invited the twins to our home for dinner. They want to know if they can spend the night with our boys."

"Can we, Daddy?" they chimed in unison.

He smiled down at them and ruffled their hair. "Of course."

They ran off, dragging Jundi with them. Keasa followed, smiling over her shoulder at Grant and Alex.

They walked into the house. The screen door slammed shut all by itself, but this time Grant closed the main door as well, then turned to the woman he loved. She moved into his arms. Wordlessly his mouth moved toward hers, capturing it gently at first, getting to know the taste of her all over again. She moaned softly when the kiss deepened and their tongues probed and explored. All the months of pent-up emotion were released in that passionate kiss. All the nights of lying awake.

He picked her up in his arms, carried her to the bedroom, and deposited her gently on the cool sheets. Then, lying next to her, he pulled her slender body against his own and molded her to him with a hand that moved sensuously down her back, over her hip to her exposed thigh.

They lay facing one another on the pillow. "Oh, I do love you," Grant said, once more drinking in the sight of her. She kissed the corners of his mouth and trailed her way to his earlobe, which she nipped gently. "And I love you." An impish smile curved her lips. "And I'll still respect you in the morning."

They kissed again, so deeply that Alex felt she was being drawn inside out. But it wasn't enough. It would never be enough. Piece by piece their clothing fell to the floor until there was nothing between them but the warmth of their bodies and the nerve-tingling friction as their flesh touched.

Grant rolled her onto her back and threw one of his legs between hers as his mouth caressed her slender neck and behind her ears, then trailed its way with exquisite slowness over her shoulder and down her arm. When he got to her wrist, his mouth moved over to the curve of her waist and across her flat stomach, then kissed a moist path to the soft swell of her breast, kissing around it in ever shrinking circles until, unable to stand it any longer, Alex tangled her fingers in his thick blond hair and pressed his mouth to her raised nipple, arching under him at the delicious wave of sensation that streamed through her.

His hand slid lightly over her body and down her side, tantalizing her. She tugged on his hair, and he left her breast to capture her mouth once more, drinking deeply of her sweetness. "Grant," she moaned, burying her face in his neck. "Don't ever let me go again. I couldn't bear it."

He kissed her damp hair. "Neither could I."

"We belong together. We always have."

He raised himself over her slightly. "We still have some problems."

"Not as far as I'm concerned."

He smiled tenderly down at her. "As of our marriage tomorrow, you will become an instant mother to two lovable but mischievous sons. Do you still say there are no problems?"

"I love them already."

His smile faded. "And what about the fact that I can never give you a child?"

Her finger trailed a path down his cheek. "You're giving me two. And I decided a long time ago that if I couldn't have your baby, I didn't want anyone's. I haven't changed my mind."

He wrapped her in his embrace. "Welcome home, my love."

She exhaled a long breath. She *was* home. With the man she loved and their family. Wherever he was, was where she belonged. Where she wanted to be.

Grant looked into her face once more and found so much love shining out at him that it took his breath away. Everything about her took his breath away. She felt him hard against her and her own desire stirred. He saw it in her eyes and felt it in the seductive movement of her body beneath his.

"Oh, no, you don't," he told her, flicking her nose and rolling onto his back, pulling her on top of him. "This is going to take the rest of the night."

Epilogue

Alexandra came out of the house and onto the porch. A year had passed. Chi, now an official member of the family after having been rejected in no uncertain terms by the wild herds, came racing out after her, her hooves comically flying in four different directions as they slid on the smooth cement of the porch.

Alex's eyes sparkled at the sight, as they always did. Then, with a sigh, she leaned her elbows on the railing and narrowed her eyes against the bright sun as she searched the sky for the new plane. Grant and the boys should be returning soon from Seronera with the week's supplies.

Keasa walked across the rope bridge and up the hill. Alex smiled at the woman who had become a dear friend. "Is school out already?"

Keasa sat on the steps and Alex joined her. "In self-defense! Those children are learning so quickly I need extra time to prepare their lessons."

Alex shook her head. "It's amazing what they've accomplished in such a short time." She patted the African woman's knee. "We did good, Keasa."

Both women grew alert at the sound of an airplane approaching. It gave Keasa a warm feeling to see the way Alex's face lit up. Alex got up and ran down the hill, stopping at the bottom, hands on her slender hips, to watch as Grant landed the plane and rolled to a stop.

Craig and Timmy tore out of the passenger side and ran to her. She laughingly caught one under each arm.

"Hey, Mom!" Timmy began.

"Timmy!" Craig glared at him. "I get to ask her."

She hugged them both to her sides, amazed at the way her feelings for these two incredible little boys had grown. They were *her* sons. She couldn't have loved them more if she'd borne them herself. "Ask me what?"

With a final glare at his brother, Craig gazed up at her. "Do you really know how to play baseball? Dad says you were on a little league team, and I say girls aren't allowed on little league teams." The word "girls" was uttered with indescribable disgust. "So how 'bout it, Mom? Can you play baseball?"

Grant came up behind her and rested his hand on the curve of her hip. "Well, Mom?" he asked close to her ear. "Answer the boy. And don't let the fact that the entire future of the women's movement hinges on your answer influence you in any way."

She kissed his cheek. "What a comfort you're going to be in my old age." Then she looked back down at the boys. "If you can find the bat and ball Grandma and Grandpa Hollister brought you last month, I'll show you—all *three* of you male chauvinists—how a *real* woman hits a baseball."

Both Craig and Timmy were skeptical, but off they ran. Grant turned Alex into his arms and smiled softly down at her. "Happy anniversary, Mrs. Adams."

She lifted her arms and tangled her fingers in his thick, blond hair. "Kiss me, Mr. Adams," she ordered huskily.

A slow smile curved his handsome mouth. "Ummmmm." He pulled her even closer. "Any place in particular?"

Her cheeks grew delightfully pink.

With a laugh, he hugged her, then shook his head as he looked down at her. "Oh, Alexandra," he said, sighing. "When you walked back into my life a year ago, I was sure I could never love you more than I did that day. I was wrong. You've become such a part of me that I don't know where I stop and you begin anymore." He raised a hand to cup her cheek. "Are you happy?"

She put her hand over his and turned her head until her lips rested against his palm. "You need to ask?"

His gaze warmed her. "No," he said quietly. "I guess I don't."

But Alex knew he wanted to hear it from her. She put a hand on either side of his face and looked deeply into his eyes. "Dr. Grant Adams. *My* Dr. Grant Adams. I've never been happier. This past year with you and our sons has been the best year of my life. And may I add that I've had some pretty good years, so we're not talking small potatoes here."

"The isolation of Banagi isn't wearing thin?"

"On the contrary. I wonder how I ever managed to survive so long in so-called civilization. Did you notice that I don't even scream at the sight of snakes anymore?"

Grant kissed her forehead and rested his

chin on top of her shining hair. The intensity of what he felt for this woman frightened him at times.

"We found them!" yelled the twins as they raced headlong down the hill, one waving a bat and the other a ball. They came to a panting halt in front of their parents.

A corner of Grant's mouth lifted. "Okay, lady. Care to put your money where your mouth is?"

"Are we talking about big bucks, or who gets to cook dinner tonight and"—she looked down at the twins—"who gets to do the dishes?"

Grant took the boys aside for a private conference. They returned a moment later. "Dinner and dishes sounds fair to us."

Alex unbuttoned the sleeves of the oxford shirt she had on and rolled them up her forearms, then rubbed her hands together before taking the bat from Timmy.

Grant watched her preparations in mock fear and said in an aside to the boys, "I think we might have a ringer here."

"Backing out so soon?" she called in a challenging voice.

"Hah! Craig, toss me the ball. You'll be the catcher," Grant told him. "Timmy, you're outfield. I'll pitch."

Alex tapped the bat tip on the ground and took up her stance. Grant narrowed his eyes on her as he readied the pitch. "You're in trouble now, woman."

The ball whizzed past her, high and out-side. She just grinned at him and tapped the bat on the ground again.

The next pitch was perfect. She swung and heard the solid crack of the wood against the ball, which soared into the air, past both Grant and Timmy. Craig's eyes grew enor-mous. "Wow!" he breathed.

When the ball finally hit the ground, three pairs of eyes turned on her in amazement. She flipped her hair back and raised her nose. "I think perhaps beef Stroganoff and a nice asparagus soufflé . . . a baked apple on the side . . ."

They were moving in on her. All three of them. She cleared her throat and lowered her nose. "Hey, fellows, this menu isn't carved in stone . . ."

They kept moving in on her. She dropped the bat and backed away from them. "Fellows . . ."

They broke into a run, and so did Alex, racing up the hill as fast as her legs would carry her. But it wasn't fast enough. Grant tackled her, hitting the ground first so that she landed laughingly on top of him. Then the twins fell on top of both of them, scream-ing with delight when Alex and Grant joined forces and tickled them.

Keasa, still sitting on the porch steps, watched the scene with a satisfied smile. There were some things in this world that were meant to be. Some families in this world who were blessed with that special something.

There were still happy endings.

Silhouette Romance

IT'S YOUR OWN SPECIAL TIME

Contemporary romances for today's women.
Each month, six very special love stories will be yours
from SILHOUETTE.

$1.75 each

☐ 100 Stanford	☐ 128 Hampson	☐ 157 Vitek	☐ 185 Hampson
☐ 101 Hardy	☐ 129 Converse	☐ 158 Reynolds	☐ 186 Howard
☐ 102 Hastings	☐ 130 Hardy	☐ 159 Tracy	☐ 187 Scott
☐ 103 Cork	☐ 131 Stanford	☐ 160 Hampson	☐ 188 Cork
☐ 104 Vitek	☐ 132 Wisdom	☐ 161 Trent	☐ 189 Stephens
☐ 105 Eden	☐ 133 Rowe	☐ 162 Ashby	☐ 190 Hampson
☐ 106 Dailey	☐ 134 Charles	☐ 163 Roberts	☐ 191 Browning
☐ 107 Bright	☐ 135 Logan	☐ 164 Browning	☐ 192 John
☐ 108 Hampson	☐ 136 Hampson	☐ 165 Young	☐ 193 Trent
☐ 109 Vernon	☐ 137 Hunter	☐ 166 Wisdom	☐ 194 Barry
☐ 110 Trent	☐ 138 Wilson	☐ 167 Hunter	☐ 195 Dailey
☐ 111 South	☐ 139 Vitek	☐ 168 Carr	☐ 196 Hampson
☐ 112 Stanford	☐ 140 Erskine	☐ 169 Scott	☐ 197 Summers
☐ 113 Browning	☐ 142 Browning	☐ 170 Ripy	☐ 198 Hunter
☐ 114 Michaels	☐ 143 Roberts	☐ 171 Hill	☐ 199 Roberts
☐ 115 John	☐ 144 Goforth	☐ 172 Browning	☐ 200 Lloyd
☐ 116 Lindley	☐ 145 Hope	☐ 173 Camp	☐ 201 Starr
☐ 117 Scott	☐ 146 Michaels	☐ 174 Sinclair	☐ 202 Hampson
☐ 118 Dailey	☐ 147 Hampson	☐ 175 Jarrett	☐ 203 Browning
☐ 119 Hampson	☐ 148 Cork	☐ 176 Vitek	☐ 204 Carroll
☐ 120 Carroll	☐ 149 Saunders	☐ 177 Dailey	☐ 205 Maxam
☐ 121 Langan	☐ 150 Major	☐ 178 Hampson	☐ 206 Manning
☐ 122 Scofield	☐ 151 Hampson	☐ 179 Beckman	☐ 207 Windham
☐ 123 Sinclair	☐ 152 Halston	☐ 180 Roberts	☐ 208 Halston
☐ 124 Beckman	☐ 153 Dailey	☐ 181 Terrill	☐ 209 LaDame
☐ 125 Bright	☐ 154 Beckman	☐ 182 Clay	☐ 210 Eden
☐ 126 St. George	☐ 155 Hampson	☐ 183 Stanley	☐ 211 Walters
☐ 127 Roberts	☐ 156 Sawyer	☐ 184 Hardy	☐ 212 Young

$1.95 each

☐ 213 Dailey	☐ 217 Vitek	☐ 221 Browning	☐ 225 St. George
☐ 214 Hampson	☐ 218 Hunter	☐ 222 Carroll	☐ 226 Hampson
☐ 215 Roberts	☐ 219 Cork	☐ 223 Summers	☐ 227 Beckman
☐ 216 Saunders	☐ 220 Hampson	☐ 224 Langan	☐ 228 King

Silhouette Romance

IT'S YOUR OWN SPECIAL TIME

Contemporary romances for today's women.
Each month, six very special love stories will be yours
from SILHOUETTE. Look for them wherever books are sold
or order now from the coupon below.

$1.95 each

☐ 229 Thornton	☐ 250 Hampson	☐ 271 Allison	☐ 292 Browning
☐ 230 Stevens	☐ 251 Wilson	☐ 272 Forrest	☐ 293 Morgan
☐ 231 Dailey	☐ 252 Roberts	☐ 273 Beckman	☐ 294 Cockcroft
☐ 232 Hampson	☐ 253 James	☐ 274 Roberts	☐ 295 Vernon
☐ 233 Vernon	☐ 254 Palmer	☐ 275 Browning	☐ 296 Paige
☐ 234 Smith	☐ 255 Smith	☐ 276 Vernon	☐ 297 Young
☐ 235 James	☐ 256 Hampson	☐ 277 Wilson	☐ 298 Hunter
☐ 236 Maxam	☐ 257 Hunter	☐ 278 Hunter	☐ 299 Roberts
☐ 237 Wilson	☐ 258 Ashby	☐ 279 Ashby	☐ 300 Stephens
☐ 238 Cork	☐ 259 English	☐ 280 Roberts	☐ 301 Palmer
☐ 239 McKay	☐ 260 Martin	☐ 281 Lovah	☐ 302 Smith
☐ 240 Hunter	☐ 261 Saunders	☐ 282 Halldorson	☐ 303 Langan
☐ 241 Wisdom	☐ 262 John	☐ 283 Payne	☐ 304 Cork
☐ 242 Brooke	☐ 263 Wilson	☐ 284 Young	☐ 305 Browning
☐ 243 Saunders	☐ 264 Vine	☐ 285 Gray	☐ 306 Gordon
☐ 244 Sinclair	☐ 265 Adams	☐ 286 Cork	☐ 307 Wildman
☐ 245 Trent	☐ 266 Trent	☐ 287 Joyce	☐ 308 Young
☐ 246 Carroll	☐ 267 Chase	☐ 288 Smith	☐ 309 Hardy
☐ 247 Halldorson	☐ 268 Hunter	☐ 289 Saunders	
☐ 248 St. George	☐ 269 Smith	☐ 290 Hunter	
☐ 249 Scofield	☐ 270 Camp	☐ 291 McKay	

SILHOUETTE BOOKS, Department SB/1

1230 Avenue of the Americas
New York, NY 10020

Please send me the books I have checked above. I am enclosing $_____
(please add 75¢ to cover postage and handling. NYS and NYC residents please
add appropriate sales tax). Send check or money order—no cash or C.O.D.'s
please. Allow six weeks for delivery.

NAME _____

ADDRESS _____

CITY _____ STATE/ZIP _____